She was lying on her side, in a twisted position, and the blood was soaking right through the mink and forming a little puddle on the sidewalk. I knelt by her side. Her eyes were glazing fast, and her face, drained of blood, looked ghostly. She looked up at me, her head lolling, and tried to say something. "Vic...."

She sank back. I threw open her coat and saw that there wasn't much use calling an ambulance. One shot had been enough. He had used a .45, and the big slug had entered right between her shoulder blades, bored through her body at tremendous force, and had emerged smack between her lovely breasts, half an inch to the right of the sternum.

There was a hole in her blouse with the diameter of a half dollar, and that hole went right through her body, heart and all. She had stayed alive for thirty seconds after the shot on sheer willpower, nothing more.

The key, I thought.

As I half expected, she was clutching it in her hand. The fingers hadn't started to get stiff yet, of course, but her grip was tight. I pried the key loose and slipped it into my pocket, and not a moment too soon, either, because the next minute the place was full of cops...

BLOOD on
the MINK

by Robert Silverberg

A HARD CASE **CRIME** NOVEL

A HARD CASE CRIME BOOK
(HCC-106)
First Hard Case Crime edition: April 2012

Published by

Titan Books
A division of Titan Publishing Group Ltd
144 Southwark Street
London
SE1 0UP

in collaboration with Winterfall LLC

Print edition ISBN 978-0-85768-768-5
E-book ISBN 978-0-85768-769-2

Design direction by Max Phillips
www.maxphillips.net

Typeset by Swordsmith Productions

The name "Hard Case Crime" and the Hard Case Crime logo
are trademarks of Winterfall LLC. Hard Case Crime books
are selected and edited by Charles Ardai.

Printed in the United States of America

Visit us on the web at www.HardCaseCrime.com

*FOR W. W. SCOTT, BUT FOR WHOM THERE'D HAVE BEEN
NO BLOOD ON THE MINK*

BLOOD ON THE MINK

ONE

It was cold out at Chicago International Airport. A chill, nasty wind was rolling in off the lake. I puffed on a butt and watched the big DC-8 come taxiing in. The three Chicago detectives grew tense.

"There she is," one of them murmured. "Flight 180, out of L.A. With Vic Lowney on board."

"Not for long," another chuckled.

I didn't say anything. It wasn't my place to make small talk. Leave that for the locals. I had a job to do, and the job began with my getting on that plane wearing Vic Lowney's name and Vic Lowney's identity. I only hoped the three locals didn't mess things up getting Lowney off the plane. One fumble, one bit of gunplay, and the whole job would be bollixed.

The DC-8 was slowing to a halt now. The ground crew went bustling out. They shoved the ramp up under the plane's door, and a moment later the passengers started getting off. A stewardess was reminding everybody, "Back in your seats in twenty minutes, please. This is only a brief stopover."

Two by two they came out. Los Angeles to Philly, via Chicago. I clicked off each face as it appeared. The twelfth man out of the plane was our man.

Lowney had a Los Angeles look about him. He was tall

and broad and heavily tanned, and he stepped off the plane with a kind of a swagger. His thick black hair was shiny with pomade. He wore a bright yellow shirt, a string tie, pegged pants, suede shoes, and—though it was a gloomy afternoon in Chi—dark sunglasses.

If he could have seen me, lounging against the wall just inside the departure shed, he would have had a shock. The faces weren't the same, but everything else was. String tie, yellow shirt, sunglasses and all. I even had my cigarette drooping at the same angle. The tan had taken me four days under the U-V lamp.

I'm sort of a chameleon that way. It's what I get paid for. Right now I was busy convincing myself that *I* was Vic Lowney, number three man of the Southern Cal crime syndicate. Inside of five minutes, I was going to have to convince the rest of the world that I was Lowney, too. And my life depended on making it come off.

The three Chi detectives flashed their badges at the airline man and moved out onto the field just as Lowney came sauntering across. He had long legs, and he wanted to stretch them a little before resuming his flight to Philadelphia. The Chi boys might have been ad men right off Wacker Avenue, with their flannels and their attaché cases. Lowney didn't suspect a thing right up until the moment they quietly surrounded him.

The whole thing took maybe fifteen seconds. They whispered to Lowney and one of them showed identification. I saw Lowney's face go icy. His lips moved in brief and probably impolite phrases. The Chi men murmured back, and one of them gently took hold of Lowney's elbow. He jerked free, and I thought there was going to be action, but the detective took the elbow again. They escorted him off the field, taking the next door down. I didn't budge. I stubbed out my cigarette and lit another.

Ten minutes went by, and then one of the detectives reappeared, smiling like a little boy with a report card full of A's. He wanted me to stick a gold star on his cheek, I guess. He said, "He's in custody."

"So?"

"Everything went smooth, no?"

"The plane's going to leave soon," I said. I'm not paid to hand out compliments to the locals. "You got anything for me?"

"Sure. Sure, right here."

He slipped me a little blue folder. Lowney's plane tickets and baggage checks. "When you get settled in Philly, go through his bags. Anything you don't need, turn over to the police. They'll ship it back here."

I scowled at him. I could figure out that much of the deal for myself. Slipping the folder into my pocket, I nodded quickly and slouched back against the wall. I didn't want to talk to him anymore.

From here on in, I was Vic Lowney.

I waited five minutes, and just before the other passengers started coming back on board I got in line with the people getting on in Chi, and passed through. I sauntered aboard the way Vic Lowney would. The stewardess gave me a pretty smile and welcomed me on board. I reminded her that I was a through passenger from L.A. That shook her up a little. The nose and the lips were all wrong, but the glasses hid the eyes, and the clothes were pretty much the same. I went to my seat. Lowney had reserved one in advance, and the stub was attached to his ticket.

The plane filled up fast. One by one, the engines started up. We moved out onto the runway.

Lowney had left an Angeleno newspaper on his seat. I picked it up and started reading about the Dodgers. A minute later, we were in the air.

I kept the paper open in front of me, but I wasn't really interested in the doings of Sherry and Snider and Gilliam. I was going over and over Vic Lowney's dossier in my mind, letting it seep into my brain until it became my own biography.

Your name is Victor Emanuel Lowney. Born 12 October 1927, Encino, California. Mother an Italian nightclub singer, Maria Buonsignore, died 1944, age 40. Father a movie bit player, Ernest Lowney, died 1932, drowning, age 30. You grew up in Pasadena, went to high school there, left in 1944 after three years. 1944–48, small-time crime. Car thefts, smuggling out of Tijuana, mostly girls. Met Charley Hammell October 1948. Originally hired as muscle, but quickly rose in the Hammell organization. For the last six years you've been his left-hand man. You have no police record, so he sends you all over the country as his personal representative. Like this trip to Philly.

You're a bachelor, and you've got a big house in Pacific Palisades. You hate filter-tip cigarettes, drink vodka mar-

tinis above anything else, and you've got a good eye for women. You eat steak for breakfast. You're hot-tempered but shrewd. You've made half a dozen kills, but nothing proven. You were rejected by the army in 1950 on account of heart palpitations, thanks to the special injection Charley Hammell's doctor gave you before your physical. In general, Vic Lowney, you're a cold-blooded louse.

I was used to being a louse. In my line of work you don't get to impersonate nice people.

You get word in Omaha or Fond du Lac or Jersey City that they need you, and next thing you know you're busy studying somebody and becoming him. Or maybe creating somebody out of whole cloth. It isn't pretty work, posing as a criminal. You swim through an ocean of filth before your job is done, and a lot of that filth gets swallowed.

But the job *has* to be done. *Somebody* has to do it.

I guess I'm the lucky one.

This time it was counterfeiting. For the past five or six months there had been a deluge of very classy queer stuff on the East Coast. Nothing but fives and tens, of course— it doesn't pay to make queer singles, while big bills attract too much attention. These fives and tens were pretty special. The engraving was downright flawless, and only the paper didn't quite measure up to Uncle Sam's own standard.

It was a close enough match, though, to fool anybody but an expert. Uncle Sam has a hard enough time keeping the budget balanced without competition from free enterprise. So the treasury men started tightening a net. It took three months to center the operation on Philadelphia. It took another two months to pick up the clue that Mr. Big of the queer-pushers was one Henry Klaus of Philadephia, a man well known by the Philly authorities but thus far able to stay on the outside of a cell.

Picking up Klaus wouldn't help much. The way to smash the ring was to nab the engraver, who was obviously a man of great talent. Only Klaus kept him well hidden, evidently. Nobody had a lead.

At this point I got alerted to move into the case. The reasoning was that only an inside operator could get hold of that engraver. I was still trying to dream up a point of entry when we picked up word that Vic Lowney of L.A. was on his way East for a powwow with Klaus. The police had their own system of underworld intelligence—otherwise they'd never do better than parking tickets. They got the word. Lowney was being sent by Charley Hammell to line up a West Coast outlet for the queer stuff.

We got the wheels in motion. A West Coast man briefed me on Lowney. I roasted under a sunlamp to give myself an Angeleno tan. We plucked Lowney off his plane midway to Philly.

And here I was, twenty thousand feet in the air, wearing padded shoulders and a brand-new suntan and the identity of a louse.

It was getting close to five, Philadelphia time, when the plane started to dip low over the City of Brotherly Love. I fastened my seatbelt and waited for the landing.

It was October, and winter was closing in fast on Pennsylvania. The sky had a dull gray look, and the temperature was in the low fifties.

I strolled off the plane and into the terminal. This was the rough point, right at the beginning. The dossier said Lowney had never been to Philadelphia and knew none of Klaus' men personally. So far as we knew, no photo had been sent. The letter we intercepted mentioned only that Lowney could be recognized by the yellow shirt, string tie, and sunglasses. But if a photo *had* been sent—

I stood near the baggage counter and lit up. Two or three minutes went by. Then I saw two guys edging up. One was six-three high, and about the same wide. The other was small and ratty-looking. They both wore heavy slouchy-looking winter clothing. I ignored them.

The big one rumbled, "Uh—Lowney?"

I looked them over. "*Mister* Lowney," I said coldly.

"Yeah. We're from Klaus."

"*Mister* Lowney."

They looked at each other. I stared right through them. The ratty one said, "Klaus sent us, *Mister* Lowney. We've got a car waiting outside."

I made no comment on that. "Where's the john in this place?" I asked.

"There's one right around that bend," the big one said.

"Are you going to call me *Mister* Lowney or do I have to report that you boys are a bunch of crude yeggs?"

The big lad glowered at me. "The washroom is right back there, *Mister* Lowney."

"Thanks," I said. I pulled my baggage claim check loose and, handed it to the ratty one. "Here. I'm going to go comb my hair. Pick up my luggage. Two Samsonite cases."

"Yes, Mr. Lowney." I could see him gagging over every syllable.

I ducked into the washroom, gave my pompadour some fresh curlicues, and leaned against the wall and looked at my watch for five minutes. Then I walked slowly out. The reception committee was waiting by the baggage counter, and the little one had his foot up on one of my suitcases. When he saw me, he got his foot off. In a hurry.

"We got your bags, Mr. Lowney."

"Okay. You want a medal?"

"Follow us, Mr. Lowney."

I let them carry my suitcases. By now they had caught the idea that I wasn't going to get chummy with underlings. We marched out through the terminal to the parking lot, and up to an Imperial sedan half a block long. Why gang boys go for these big black limousines I'll never understand. They might just as well put up a neon sign that says *Gangster*.

The little man opened the back door and I got in. Pintsize tried to get in next to me, but I shooed him away with my foot.

"You sit in front, man."

The beady eyes were marbles of hate. "Now listen here, tough guy—"

"I said you sit in front. Want to debate it with me?"

His face unstiffened. He walked around to the front

seat and got in next to the big one. I had taken the first round on points, by plenty.

"I'm staying at the Penn Plaza," I said.

"We're supposed to take you to Klaus."

"You take me to the Penn Plaza. You think I flew three thousand miles to run right into a business conference? Wise up, simps. I need some relaxing first."

"Klaus is gonna be awful mad—"

"I'll see him when I feel like seeing him."

The big boy turned around and said in a feathery voice, "Hey, *Mister* Lowney, you talk like you did us a big favor by coming here. You oughta realize that *we're* the guys who gonna do *you* the favor."

I gave him one cold look that wiped the smugness off his face.

"Can it, friend," I said quietly. "Are you going to take me to the Penn Plaza, or do I take a cab?"

TWO

The Penn Plaza was a brand new hotel, maybe a year old, on Market a couple of blocks from City Hall. It was all shiny glass and steel, and single rooms began at eighteen bucks a night, and in general it was the sort of place that a Los Angeles man might be expected to stay at.

I let Klaus' two thugs drag my suitcases out of the sedan's trunk and turn them over to a bellhop. Then I said to them, "You tell Klaus he can get in touch with me here. He can try calling any time except between two and ten in the morning. Tell him I'm not available for business meetings until tomorrow."

The muscle looked rueful. "Klaus, he was looking forward to a meet with you tonight," the little one said.

"I'll see him tomorrow."

I walked into the hotel.

There were no snags about the reservations Lowney had made. They gave me a nice enough room on the tenth floor. I freshened up and was getting dressed for dinner when the phone rang. I picked it up.

"Mr. Lowney?"

"That's right."

"This is Don Minton. I'm Mr. Klaus' assistant."

"What is it, Minton?"

"The chauffeur tells us you're not available for a meet tonight. Mr. Klaus is a little disappointed."

"Let me talk to him."

"I'm sorry, Mr. Lowney. Mr. Klaus is unavailable at the moment. But he asks me to convey to you his regret that no meeting is feasible this evening. He wonders if you'll reconsider. He had made dinner reservations, you see, and he's looking forward—"

"Tell Mr. Klaus," I said cuttingly, "that Mr. Lowney is busy this evening. You got that?"

"Yes, Mr. Lowney." Everything very polite and deferential, but I could feel the anger underneath. "I'll tell him that. And when do you think a meeting might be arranged, Mr. Lowney?"

"Say, tomorrow. Tomorrow at six."

"Very good, Mr. Lowney. I'll pick you up at six sharp."

"Don't rush," I said. "I'm a slow dresser."

Minton gave me a frosty little heh-heh-heh and hung up. I got out of the yellow shirt and such, and put on something out of Lowney's wardrobe. We were practically the same size, which made things very convenient. I took a leisurely glance through his suitcases, but there was nothing there but clothes and stuff, and some spare rounds for the gun he was carrying.

Around seven, I went down for dinner. The hotel had three or four restaurants, but I picked the most expensive. Hell, it wasn't *my* money. And it was in keeping with Lowney's character, anyway.

Lowney had a weakness for steak. A relief, that was—if

the dossier had mentioned that he ate nothing but lob-ster, I'd have had to eat lobster, and I hate lobster. But I didn't mind loading up on steak as part of the act. I put away a pound or so of rare sirloin, prefacing the meal with a couple of vodka martinis and accompanying it with a nice little bottle of wine. California wine, of course. Lowney had a liking for the good life, but he was a patriot at heart. No Châteauneuf-du-Pape for *him*, just good honest Napa red wine.

As I left the restaurant, some quail fluttered down toward me. Everything about her shrieked that she was a fancy pro. Gold lamé dress that ended well below the armpits and showed lots of softly rounded pale flesh. Un-likely blonde hair. Full red lips, only slightly too hard. Calculating greenish eyes. "Mr. Lowney?"

"That's my name, honey. What can I do for you?"

"You've got it wrong, Mr. Lowney. Maybe *I* can do something for *you*," she murmured huskily.

Now, the Penn Plaza is a reputable place, and I was sure it didn't supply floozies for the clientele. I gave her a puzzled look and she explained, "Mr. K. sent me over. He thought you might be lonely, this being a strange town and all."

"How thoughtful of him."

"We could go to dance for a while," she said hopefully. "Or maybe a show. And then—"

Either in or out of character, I couldn't see very much about this girl that I didn't find easy to look at. But the deal she was offering didn't fit in with my plans. Klaus was apparently interested in keeping tabs on me while I was in Philly. If he couldn't see me himself this first night, he was sending some choice flesh over to make sure I didn't get out of sight.

I shook my head, and, believe me, it hurt to do it. "Sorry," I said.

"What do you mean, *sorry*?"

"I appreciate the offer. But it so happens I've got a business appointment tonight. You can tell that to Mr. K."

She looked stunned. I guess she wasn't used to having an offer of free merchandise turned down. "What about afterward?" she purred.

"Afterward, I sleep," I said. "I need my rest, baby. You go thank Mr. K. for his consideration. Also tell him I'm engaged elsewhere tonight." I took a tenspot from my wallet and handed it to her. "Here. This is for your taxi fare home. Maybe we'll make it some other time, huh?"

"Yeah. Sure, Mr. Lowney. Whenever you like." She glided away. I shook my head regretfully. But business came before pleasure, and I wanted to keep Klaus worried. I didn't want him to get the idea he had any monopoly on my negotiating time while I was in Philadelphia. So I blotted all thought of those appealing snowy hillocks out of my mind, and went downstairs to the lobby.

Philadelphia is not exactly the most interesting town in the world, but it could be worse. I sauntered out for a little stroll around town. I walked down to Broad, looked in store windows for a while, and then—after making sure I wasn't being tailed—got into a cab.

"Just drive," I told the cabbie. "Take me on a nice big zigzag, and when the meter reads three bucks let me off wherever I happen to be."

He dropped me finally in a shabby suburb about three miles north of City Hall. I walked to the corner, turned it, and found a movie theater. I went in, sat down, watched a western for an hour, and left. I took a cab back to the Penn Plaza.

Let Klaus think I had had a rendezvous with some other local gangland figure. Let him sweat a little.

I got back to my room at quarter after eleven. I changed into one of Lowney's ornate silk dressing-gowns, ordered a vodkatini as a nightcap from room service, and sacked out by midnight. It hadn't been a very eventful day. I had switched places with Lowney. I had come to Philadelphia, and I had impressed on Klaus and his bunch that I was not a man to be trifled with. And I had blocked a pass thrown by a lovely blonde. Regrettable, but unavoidable. The *next* time Klaus waved a woman in front of my nose, though....

Morning. I phoned for my breakfast: small cut of tenderloin, rare, french fries, glass of milk. A weird way to begin the day, but that was Lowney's way. Luckily, I had the stomach for it.

I lounged around the hotel all day. At six on the button, the room phone rang. It was Minton. Was I ready to come down for supper? I told him to wait ten minutes. I kept him waiting twenty.

He was pacing around in the lobby, a dapper, Ivy League

type around thirty, short and crew-clipped and impatient. The beady-eyed one who had met me at the airport was with him. Minton bustled out and gave me the big hand-shake. Beady-eyes said nothing.

"The car's outside," Minton said.

It was the same black limousine, with the same big goon behind the wheel. I had expected to find Klaus in it, but he wasn't. Minton and I got in the back.

"Is Klaus meeting us at the restaurant?" I asked.

Minton smiled. "He'll be with us later."

"Can't he demean himself to eat with me?"

"Something urgent came up this afternoon."

I got the pitch. I had been grinding salt in the Klaus bunch's eyes, and Klaus was trying to give some of my own stuff back to me. Well, I couldn't blame him. He had scored a point in the little fencing match.

I wasn't keen on eating with underlings, but I couldn't back out of it now. So I simply didn't talk. I concentrated on eating, and answered Minton's polite phrases with curt nods. He gave up, after a while. We ran up a seventy-buck check for the four of us, and I let Minton pick it up without even offering. He had to take care of the tip, too. By the time we got back into the car, he looked like that nice fancy meal was curdling in his intestines. But a man like Lowney didn't pal it with Mintons: I had to make that clear.

"We going to Klaus now?" I asked.

"Yes," Minton said, as though the single syllable cost him a month's pay.

The limousine pulled up in front of the Hotel Burke on 16th Street, and we had a nice thirty-story ride up to the penthouse suite. Klaus did things in style, as he could well afford with presses running night and day turning out the queer.

He was surrounded by a dozen of his men, only a couple of them goons and the rest college types. Klaus himself was a man of about fifty, short and stockily built, with lank gray hair combed straight across and drooping over his right ear. His nose was a straggly beak; his eyes were blue-gray, and chilly. We shook hands, and he gave me a piercing glance.

"So very good to see you, Mr. Lowney. We've heard so much about you on the East Coast."

"M-G-M wants to film the story of my life," I said. "We're dickering on the price."

Klaus chuckled. "Very funny, Mr. Lowney I'm sure it will make a fascinating movie. You must send me tickets to the premiere."

"I'll do that," I promised. "I'll be honored to have you come. With or without your retinue."

"Does it seem crowded here, Mr. Lowney?"

"Just a mite."

"Perhaps we can go into the next room—"

We went into an inner office. Minton trailed along like the good lackey he was. Klaus suggested drinks, and I sent Minton scurrying off to mix vodka martinis.

For the next half hour we sat around like old buddies,

swapping the latest news of our respective domains. He fed me East Coast gossip and I let him in on various West Coast matters that Lowney could be expected to be privy to. Then we talked about the stock market for a while. Klaus was heavily invested in electronics companies, and he was wondering what to do. I told him to take his profits and get into oil. Real chummy stuff.

When I got tired of the routine I said quite casually, "I'd like to see a sample of your product, Mr. Klaus."

"Oh, let's not get down to business so soon, Mr. Lowney. Have another cocktail."

"I'd rather not," and suddenly there was steel in my voice. "Let's see the bills."

A shadow of a frown crossed Klaus' well-groomed face. Turning easily to Minton, he said, "Get a couple of packages, Don. One of fives, one of tens."

Minton went into an adjoining room and came back with two little stacks of bills, one hundred of each kind, bound around their middles with blue paper. He tossed them down on the desk in front of me.

I picked up the tens and riffled through them without breaking the band. They were new and crisp, and they had the feel of money. The smell, too. They weren't limp and floppy like some phony stuff. They had the feel of engravings, not cheap litho stuff. The serial numbers were clear and sharp, and ran in sequence.

Breaking the band, I took a tenspot off the top and held it gingerly between my fingertips. It was good.

It was *damned* good.

It was a Federal Reserve Note on the Philadelphia bank. The green seal on the right was prefect, as was the Federal Reserve emblem on the left. In between was the portrait of Hamilton, and that was flawless too. There were no breaks in the cross-hatching behind the head, nor any awkwardness about the shading of the face. The lathework around the margins of the bill was all it had to be. On the flip side, the picture of the Treasury Building had been copied by the hand of a master. For an uneasy moment I wondered if Klaus might be pulling a con by showing me a pack of real bills.

I looked over the fives. They were lovely. Whoever had engraved this queer stuff had as much skill as anybody working for the Bureau of Engraving and Printing.

Klaus and Minton were waiting for my verdict. I took a long, slow look at both sets of bills. If they had rung in real Government stuff on me, I was going to make one hell of a fool out of myself.

It was a chance I had to take.

Klaus couldn't stand it any longer. He broke the sticky silence.

"Well, Mr. Lowney? What is your opinion of our handi-work?"

I moistened my lips. Tapping the stack of tens, I said, "Not bad at all, Klaus. Not bad at all. Of course, they're a long way from being perfect. You've got to admit that yourself. I don't know if I can make a deal for a product of this grade."

THREE

It was as though I'd smacked him across the bridge of the nose with a billy-club. His face went pale and his eyes blazed with surprise and anger.

The reaction told me they hadn't rung in real stuff as a gimmick. If they had, they'd have been laughing themselves silly. Instead, they were boiling mad.

Klaus' mouth became a tight little line. Minton burst out, "Look here, Lowney, you've been trying to cut us down since you got off that plane. You know goddamn well this is the best queer that can be made."

"I say it's bush league stuff. You might as well be turning it out on a mimeograph."

Klaus was doing a slow simmer. But Minton was really sore. Maybe he was supposed to be demonstrative for the two of them. Anyway, he got halfway out of his seat, his lips working. I gave him a little twist of the blade.

"If I had known the stuff was crud like this, I could have sent my chauffeur east to look at it."

"Why, you arrogant punk, you ought to—" Minton began, getting the rest of the way out of his seat. He started to take a poke at me. I slipped a left past his guard and splattered his lips. Klaus didn't budge. Minton staggered back a little, his Ivy League phiz a bit battered now, and his hand went into his breast pocket.

I kicked my chair back and came at him. I hit him in the belly just as the gun appeared; all the life went out of him, and I caught the gun hand, twisted, nodded as the .38 fell to the thick carpet.

Minton looked ready to explode. He tried to get loose and took a feeble poke at me. I ducked it and smashed him hard, right under his lower lip.

He sat down on the carpet. His eyes looked glassy, and there were droplets of blood on his nice white shirt. I picked up the .38, put it on the table next to the phony dough, and sat down again. I hadn't even worked up a sweat.

"Your man is kind of impetuous, Klaus."

"He's a fool. Get up, Minton!" Klaus snapped. Minton hauled himself uncertainly to his feet. "Now get out of here and clean yourself up!"

Minton slithered out. I wondered if he had put on the act on a signal from Klaus. The product had been defended, in an incompetent sort of way. Now negotiations could proceed. I had the feeling that Klaus was unhappy about the way things were going.

He said in an oily voice, "I apologize for the unpleasantness of my colleague, Mr. Lowney. You see, we all take a rather staunch pride in our product. What exactly is your objection to it? Surely the engraving can stand any scrutiny whatever, and—"

"The engraving's fine," I said. "It's the paper."

"The best available."

"Not good enough. I believe in being frank, Klaus. I'm

disappointed in the product. I'm going to call Hammell and tell him so."

"Don't be hasty. Maybe we can discuss improvements."

"Let me call Hammell first. Mind if I use your phone?"

It was a transcontinental call, but he didn't bat an eye. He shoved the phone across the desk to me. I picked it up and gave the long distance operator an Exeter number in L.A. It wasn't Hammell I was calling, of course. It was a prearranged pickup in L.A. It was my way of letting HQ know that I had arrived safely and made rendezvous with Klaus.

Someone answered and I said, "Give me Hammell." That was part of the signal. Asking for Hammell meant, *Not alone, possibly someone on an extension, so play along.* Asking for "Charley" would have meant relative safety.

A gruff voice said, "Hammell here. What's the scoop, Vic?"

"I'm at Klaus' and I've seen the queer. I'm not bowled over."

"How so?"

"The paper tips it off. The stuff could be a lot better, that's for sure."

"You want to call the deal off?"

"Not unless you do. Maybe I can goose them a little. The product isn't hopeless."

"Yeah, you do that. Keep in touch, man."

"Will do, Charley."

I hung up. HQ knew I was in business, now. I turned back to Klaus and said, "He wants me to negotiate."

"We aren't hopeless, eh?"

"Not quite." I took a crisp new real tenspot out of my wallet and laid it alongside one of the phonies. The bills looked like twins. Only an expert could detect with his naked eye the minute difference in paper qualities. Privately I was impressed. But I didn't let my impression show. "You're turning out some fair stuff, Klaus. But you'll have to pick up the grade a little. Select your paper more carefully. I want an exact match."

"We aren't the Government, Mr. Lowney."

"You've got to be damn close." I rose, casually peeling ten tens and ten fives off the stacks of queer. "I'll take these for reference. Suppose you get in touch with me in a couple of days and let me see your latest products. The T-men are sharp out in our country, Klaus."

"You don't want to talk terms now?"

"Not till I've seen the product I can buy."

"You're a very difficult man, Mr. Lowney."

"I'm paid to be difficult, Klaus. Will you show me out?"

On the way out I noticed a girl. She obviously belonged to Klaus, and had been elsewhere in the suite when I arrived. She was an auburn-haired five-eighter, which made her a shade or two taller than Klaus. I pegged her for twenty-eight. She wore a lemon-colored gown and filled it out more than adequately. The word that summed her up was *lush*.

She gave me a sizzling look and murmured to Klaus, "Is this your California friend, honeybear?"

"Yes." Klaus wasn't in a conversational mood.

"Why don't you intro*duce* us, loverbug?" she purred.

Klaus looked displeased. "Vic Lowney, Miss Carol Champlain." End of introduction. He said curtly to me, "I'll be in touch with you in a couple of days, Mr. Lowney. Or you can get in touch with me here at the Burke."

"Ye-ah," Champlain drawled. *"Do* keep in touch."

I gave her a nice smile, flashed a businessman's grin at Klaus, and headed for the elevator. As I closed the door I caught a glimpse of a puffy-faced Minton glaring at me. I guess he was about to get a dressing-down from Klaus for bungling things and pulling the gun.

I stepped out into a misty, cold autumn night and hailed a cab. Klaus hadn't even offered to have me driven home. I suppose he was a little sore.

And he had every right to be, because his product was fabulous. Only it wasn't good tactics to say so. Not right away.

I figured he wouldn't sleep so well tonight. Not even with that bosomy redhead to keep him warm.

Back in my room at the Penn Plaza, I took out Klaus' bills and looked them over. They were really extra special. The paper, despite my quibbling, was a close enough match to fool nine out of ten bank tellers and ninety-eight out of a hundred storekeepers.

But the engraving was the real feature. You have to make engraved plates if you want to get away with faking U.S. currency. Any sort of photo-offset job will be immediately apparent to anyone but a novice. The trouble is that banknote engraving is an art and a science both. There aren't many capable engravers in this country, and those there are are well known and well watched. The Secret Service took care of the possibility that Government engravers might want to peddle a few plates on the side.

Whoever Klaus was using, the fellow was good. In capital letters. So long as Klaus had these plates—or the man who made them—he could easily dump ten million dollars' worth of bad bills a year. Or ten billion. It was all a mere matter of distribution and dispersion.

I put the bills away carefully—I didn't want to spend them by accident—and started to get ready for bed. It had been a fruitful night, I felt. Contact had been made, and I had established an image of Lowney in Klaus' eyes that probably came close to reality. Lowney's reputation was not one of genteel politeness. He was a tough son of a bitch, and he wouldn't jump into any quick deals. Klaus wasn't really expecting him to.

I was pondering the desirability of a midnight martini when the phone rang. "Hello?"

"Mr. Lowney?"

"Yeah. Who's this?"

"You wouldn't know me. My name's Litwhiler and I'm from New York. I've been trying to reach you all night."

"I've been out. What's the scoop?"

"I've got a business deal to discuss, Mr. Lowney. I'm right down here in the Penn Plaza cocktail lounge. Maybe you could come down and have a drink on me?"

"It's late. What about tomorrow?"

"I'd rather make it tonight, Mr. Lowney. Philadelphia isn't the safest town in the world for me."

I raised an eyebrow thoughtfully. "Okay, I'll be down in five minutes. How will I know you?"

"I'm in the far left-hand corner, sitting next to the fountain. I've got a charcoal gray suit on. Just walk in and look around, and I'll spot you."

I didn't know any Litwhilers, except one who used to play baseball a while ago, but I was always willing to meet somebody new. Especially somebody who had a business deal to discuss with Vic Lowney.

He stood up and waved to me the moment I entered the dim cocktail lounge—which meant he didn't know Lowney personally, but was only guessing that the big guy in western-looking clothes was his man. Litwhiler himself was of the new school of hoods, like Minton—the well-groomed kind in the sedate Brooks Brothers suit. He was a little old for the Ivy League, maybe forty, but he had a slick, sharp-edged New York look about him.

We shook hands and he said, "What are you drinking?"

"Vodkatinis." I was getting sick of them.

He ordered a couple. Then he said in a low, you-and-me kind of voice, "Let's put our cards on the table right at the outset, Mr. Lowney. We can do each other a whole lot of good."

"You don't get through to me, man."

"Give me time. I know why you're in Philly."

"Really?"

He nodded smugly. "You're here to arrange West Coast distribution of a product manufactured here."

"You must have very big ears, Mr. Litwhiler."

"I've got a very good intelligence system. When Vic Lowney flies to Philly, I find out why. I won't even ask you to confirm what I just said. I *know.*"

"Keep talking," I said noncommittally.

He fished the lemon peel out of his drink, deposited it in the ashtray, and went on, "I happen to represent a firm that's in substantially the same line as the firm you're here to deal with—the, shall we say, *K* firm. Here's an example of our merchandise."

I took a deep sip of the cocktail before I deigned to look at the ten-dollar bill he put on the formica tabletop. It was pretty crude stuff. The paper was okay, as good as Klaus', but the ink had a gloss to it that didn't really belong, and the engraving couldn't begin to match the job on the bills I had upstairs. I looked at it for a long moment. Then I said simply, "It stinks."

"Exactly, Mr. Lowney," Litwhiler said, smiling.

"Then why bother me about it?"

"Can I trouble you for your criticisms?"

"The ink's off shade, for one. And the engraving is punk. Maybe you could fool a couple of guys with this, but not me. Not me, Litwhiler, or my boss."

"We don't plan to. The ink problem is correctible. But we don't intend to use these plates any longer than we have to."

"Meaning what?"

"Meaning," he said, "that we'd like to obtain the services of the engraver for the K firm and use him ourselves. And then we'd do a comparable job."

I drummed the table impatiently. "Get to the point, Litwhiler. You're boring me."

He didn't react. "The point is this: you can get buddy-buddy with Klaus. You can find out where his engraver is. Then you can lead us to him. We'll spirit the man up to New York and have him do plates for *us*."

"Why should I doublecross Klaus to help your outfit?"

Now Litwhiler smiled. "Because we'll guarantee a price fifteen percent lower than the best Klaus can do. And $25,000 cash to you for your services. It's only good business, Lowney."

"*Mister* Lowney," I rapped.

"Sorry. But how do you feel about it?"

"I haven't talked terms with Klaus yet."

"Whenever you do. We guarantee to undercut him. We want those plates, Mr. Lowney. And/or the engraver. And you can get him for us."

I leaned back and stretched. "I'll think it over. My boss always has an eye out for cost-cutting."

"This is one chance he shouldn't pass up."

"Where can I get in touch with you, Litwhiler?"

He gave me a card. It bore the address of a jewelry firm on 47th Street in Manhattan. "Ask for Harold," he said. "That's me. I'll be driving back to New York tonight. Klaus would flay me if he ever caught me here alone."

I told him I'd be in touch, and went back upstairs. News traveled fast in the underworld. I was accustomed to that. But I hadn't expected this.

So it was a tug-of-war for the engraver, eh? With Lit-whiler tugging from New York, Klaus from Philly. And me for the U.S. Government. Three-way tugs are always interesting. I just hoped the engraver didn't get pulled apart in the process.

FOUR

The next morning, I phoned New York, doing some checking. Headquarters had no line on this Litwhiler, but when I described the phony tenner they got excited: They had seen plenty of it in their area, and they were keen on shutting off the flow. I told them I'd keep my eyes open and see what turned up.

In a way, the Litwhiler sort of counterfeit currency is nastier than the Klaus kind. The Klaus bills were good enough to fool the banks; once the stuff got into circulation, it could keep on passing until it wore out, and nobody would be cheated except Uncle Sam.

But the Litwhiler bills would get stopped at the bank window about half the time. Which meant that the shopkeepers and restaurant owners and just plain people who had been passed the queer were out the ten bucks. When the government confiscates phony money, it doesn't make good the loss to the unfortunate possessor thereof.

Not that the Klaus kind was virtuous, mind you. Klaus was cheating those shopkeepers just as thoroughly, only he was being indirect about it.

After breakfast, I got out of the hotel for some air. I guess it's about my only hobby—lonely walks through big cities. The weather was milder, and a lot of people were out. Businessmen and pretty girls and grifters and cons, all moving through the streets purposefully and rapidly. While I strolled. It's lonely work, this undercover stuff. You don't make any friends in your line of work, and you don't feel much like making them after hours, because you can't confide in anybody.

That *means* anybody. My own mother didn't know what line of work I specialized in.

You can cross off a wife and kids, too. This kind of life is too impermanent to risk leaving widows around. You don't get mixed up with steady girls, either.

You're a man with a million identities—which really means you have no identity at all. You look at yourself in the mirror and you see eyes and a nose and a mouth, but they don't really add up to a face, because to have a face you have to be a person. A solid, substantial person. Not just a guy who plays thirty different parts a year.

Not that I feel sorry for myself. It's not a bad life. Just a risky one. And dirty. You hang out with crumbs and killers and leeches, and you try to be one of them. Not be *like* them, but *be* them. And that old question keeps coming back: *Why me?* And the old answer, too. *Somebody's got to be the one.*

And the job has its rewards, too. Like when I got back to the Penn Plaza in time for lunch and had a bellhop scuttle up to me and say, "Mr. Lowney?"

"That's right."

"There's been a girl here all morning to see you. She says she'll stay here until you come back."

I frowned. "Where is she now?"

"Sitting over there by the checkout desk. I'll tell her you've come in."

"Never mind," I said. "I'll tell her myself."

I walked over, wondering what the hell was unfolding now. Let a bigwig like Lowney come to town and they flock around him like moths to a candle.

The girl was sitting with her legs crossed, and she was staring off into space and nibbling her cuticles. They were okay legs. She was an okay girl. But young. Twenty-five at tops. She had frilly blonde hair that looked natural, big blue eyes and the longest eyelashes ever.

She was dressed demurely, high-neck cashmere sweater, plaid skirt, tan trenchcoat. The sweater was nicely stuffed with goodies, nothing voluminous but a long way from being skimpy. The overall impression was a virginal one. A sweet kid, you know. The kind you like to have as your sister.

I said, "I understand you're looking for Vic Lowney."

She gave a start. "Yes. Yes, that is right. Are you he?" She spoke stiffly, with the trace of an unfamiliar accent.

"I'm Vic Lowney."

"I am Elena Szekely," she announced, getting to her feet. She was chin-high on me. She looked scared. "Let us go to your room, shall we? Right away?"

"You believe in the direct approach, don't you?"

She colored prettily. "I do not mean—to *do* anything. But talk. I must talk with you. And not being seen."

"It's pretty dark in the cocktail lounge—"

"No. Upstairs is safer. More private."

I'm not one to carry an argument too far. We headed toward the bank of elevators, and rode upstairs in silence. I let her into the room. She wriggled off the trenchcoat, threw it on a chair, and sucked in a deep breath with the obvious intention of enhancing her figure. Cooperatively, I gave her sweater an admiring glance. She flushed again; she was trying hard as hell to be a *femme fatale,* but the part just didn't ride naturally on her.

"There is no one else in the room?" she asked worriedly.

"Guaranteed."

She came up to me and put her hands on my wrists. "Mr. Lowney, you must swear to me you will not repeat to Klaus what I am about to say. Will you swear it?"

"I can keep my mouth shut."

"You must! Or Klaus will hurt me. And my father." I eased free of her embrace and pulled out a chair for her.

"Suppose you tell me why you're here, Miss—"

"Szekely," she said as I stumbled. "It is an Hungarian name. I am born in Hungary. I live in this country only a few years. My father and I come here in 1957—after the revolution—"

"And what is it you want with me?"

"To help. To help my father and me."

"You're not making yourself clear, Miss Szekely."

"My father—he is an engraver. Very, how you say?— skilled. He does postage stamps when he lived in Hungary. Also banknotes. Especially banknotes."

Miss Elena Szekely suddenly took on a new and gleaming interest for me. I told her to say more.

"We live there all during the War. It is not so bad, for we hope someday the Germans will go. I am small child then anyway. But we get Russians when the Germans go. You know about our uprising in 1956?"

"I've heard of it," I said.

"I am—the name?—Freedom Fighter. The Russians send tanks. We are defeated, and my father and I flee to Austria. In Europe there is always employment for a man with skill. We can no longer stay in Hungary. We want to go to the United States.

"In Vienna we meet a man, an American. He will send us to the United States, he says. We go as refugees. He sends us to this city, to Philadelphia. He pays all our passage. His name, it is Klaus."

The picture started to take shape. "Go on."

"We are in America a month. I know a little English, my father none. Klaus comes back from Europe and he comes to us. He shows us an American money bill. He says to my father, Can you draw this? You know—make a plate." The girl gestured angrily. "Criminals we are not, Mr. Lowney. I translate and my father refuses. Klaus makes ugly face. He tells my father to do his wishes or otherwise."

"Or otherwise what?"

"We do not know. Hurt us, perhaps. Or send us back to Hungary. What happens is this: Klaus takes my father and puts him in a house and gives him engraving tools. He tells my father to do his bidding or they will take me and—and—" She reddened. "And treat me cruelly.

"For a long time he refuses. But one day Klaus has no more patience. He takes me in front of my father, and they begin taking my clothes off, and when I am naked above the waist my father begins to cry, and—" She lowered her voice and looked at the floor. "Since that day he works for them."

"And a very good engraver he is, too."

"But a prisoner! Oh, Mr. Lowney, you must help us!"

"What kind of help do you mean?"

Her eyes grew moist. "An aunt I have in Florida, also a refugee. My father wants to live with his sister there. But Klaus guards him day and night. He does not let him go anywhere. Not even to write a letter. And I too, he watches. If we go to the police, Klaus will kill us, he says. We beg him to let us go, but they do not listen."

"And I'm supposed to do what?"

"You are a very important man, Mr. Lowney. This morning Klaus was at our house, and he and his friends talked about you. They are very anxious to please you. I think you they are afraid of. They would listen to you. You could ask them to let my father free."

"Klaus wouldn't ever agree to that."

"You could tell him," she said excitedly, "that he will make more plates for him, only in Florida. Whenever Klaus needs a plate, he can send a man to Florida and my father will make it. Only let us be free. Let us go to our people. This is supposed to be the land of the free," she said bitterly. "But we are prisoners here."

I was silent a moment. Then I said, "Klaus won't listen to me."

"He will! I know he will!"

"Let his most valuable asset get away from him? Don't be silly, girl."

"You would at least try. You would at least ask."

"What for?"

"For me. For my father. Because you are an American and it is wrong to keep him that way."

I flashed a cynical smile. "Lofty sentiments don't cut much ice, honey. I don't see the sense of asking Klaus for a favor that big."

"I will repay you," she said suddenly. "If you talk to Klaus—if he frees my father—"

I frowned, looking a little dubious, and next thing I knew she was on the floor in front of me with her arms around my knees, and her face was flaming red, and she was trying to sound like Eva Gabor as she whispered huskily, "I will give you—anything. Anything I have would be yours. I am not ugly. I would spend a night with you— a week—but talk to Klaus for me. For my father. And I will give you what no man has had yet from me."

I don't make a practice of despoiling virgins, but it would have been simple rudeness not to seem at least interested by the offer. I tugged her arms loose and lifted her to her feet. She stared up at me, scared but game, probably wondering if I planned to ask for payment in advance, right on the spot.

I said gently, "I'll see what I can do, Elena."

"You will not joke?"

"I will not joke. I'll talk to Klaus."

"And afterward—"

"And afterward we'll see."

"When will you talk to him?"

"Give me some time. Let me see how much influence I've got with him. And don't worry about a thing, Elena. I'm with you. I'll get your old man loose from Klaus."

"You are so very kind," she whispered. And then—as a kind of promissory note—she put her arms round my neck and stood up on tiptoe and kissed me. Her lips were cold. I pulled her toward me, and I could feel her heart thumping back of that virginal bosom, and I gave her the sort of kiss Lowney would be likely to give. When I let go of her, she slithered back, threw me a frightened little smile, and was gone like a shot.

I wiped the lipstick off. And scowled at my reflection in the mirror.

So the engraver was a captive Hungarian refugee? Interesting, I thought. Klaus was fully capable of such a stunt. I felt a little sick at the thought of Elena Szekely running around offering to sleep with a slick hood from the Coast just to get her father released.

All kinds of possibilities presented themselves. I felt sorry for the girl, though. Somebody who had put her life on the line for so-called freedom, only to find that America wasn't quite the paradise of liberty she'd been led to believe—Elena Szekely deserved better of the world than to live under Henry Klaus' thumb.

No wonder she was willing to sleep with Lowney. After what she and her father had been through in life, a little thing like losing her virginity wouldn't matter if it could finally guarantee them the freedom they wanted so badly.

Well, maybe Vic Lowney would take advantage of her, but I wouldn't. You've got to have some shred of decency, after all. But I figured she could be very helpful to me. Now I had my first link with the engraver—the key man in the whole caper.

FIVE

I had lunch. A light one. I was on my coffee when a bellhop came over and said, "Mr. Lowney?"

"You guessed it."

"Phone call for you. Want to take it at the table?"

"Why not?"

He brought me a plug-in phone. I picked up the receiver and a soft, throaty, purring voice said, "Hello, Vic?"

"Yeah. Who's this?"

"You mean you don't recognize the voice?"

"I guess I'm slow today. Who?"

"Carol Champlain."

I frowned. What did Klaus' girlfriend want with me? "Yeah?" I said. "What is it?"

"Listen," she said, "are you free tonight?"

"What's the pitch?"

"Klaus is going out of town. He won't be back till tomorrow. And he's leaving me behind. So that gives me the night off. I want to talk to you."

"About what?"

"Mutual aid. You free? I'll come to your hotel around nine."

"This on the level?" I asked.

"Absolutely," she breathed. "Okay?"

"Okay," I said.

I put down the phone, not knowing what it was all about but willing to listen. I didn't trust Klaus, so why should I trust his chick? But maybe she had something worth my while to hear. It never pays to say no.

Especially to a dame built the way that one was.

I had nothing much to do for the rest of the afternoon. For the sake of keeping things moving along, I phoned Klaus at his suite around four o'clock. He was getting ready to go out of town, Minton told me, so at least that much of Carol's story was kosher.

"Let me talk to him anyway," I said. "Just for a minute."

"He doesn't want to be dis—"

"Let me talk to him."

I could practically feel Minton glaring at me over the wire. But he backed down, and a moment later I heard the voice of Klaus himself greeting me none too warmly.

"I just want to tell you I've been thinking over the product you showed me last night, Klaus," I said. "Despite everything we can still do business "

"Glad to hear it. What's your bid?"

"Five cents on the dollar," I said

There was a long moment of silence at the other end. Then Klaus said, "You must be nuts."

"Five cents. Take it or leave it "

"Listen, Lowney, what we've got to offer is as good as the real thing. I could get ten times your bid without raising a sweat."

"I'd like to see you," I said. No queer-passer will work

on that slim a profit margin. The risks are too great. "A nickel's the bid."

"Why don't you offer me two cents, while you're at it?" he jeered. "Listen, Lowney, you go away somewhere and think it over some more. When you're ready to make a real bid, you let me know."

"You heard my bid," I said.

"Sure, I heard it. And you know what you can do with it, don't you?"

"Never mind," I said.

I hung up. I hadn't expected him to accept the bid, of course. But I had to begin negotiations somewhere. And the lower the better, I figured. The longer I could keep him on the string, the more time I would have for snooping around finding out the things I had to know.

I relaxed away the rest of the afternoon in front of the TV set in my room, and had a hearty dinner downstairs in the hotel dining room. Afterwards I returned to my room, got out of my clothes and into a pair of lounging pajamas and a silk dressing gown, and sat down to wait for Carol Champlain to show up.

I waited. As patiently as I knew how.

The evening ticked away. A little before nine, there was a knock on the door, very gentle, very soft. I opened it carefully.

"Hi," Carol said.

She slithered inside. I locked and chained the door as she got out of her jacket. Underneath she was wearing what must have been simple clothes for her—a clinging, exotic sheath that stunningly molded the supple contours of her breasts and thighs and buttocks. Her full red lips glistened in a kissable way.

But we eyed each other like people who couldn't fully trust each other, which we were at the moment. She said finally, "If Klaus knew I had come here, he'd kill me. Let's hope I wasn't trailed."

"Would he kill me too?"

"He's probably going to do that anyway," she said casually. "Get us some drinks, will you?"

"Such as?"

"Bourbon'll do just fine."

I phoned room service, asked them to send up a fifth of bourbon, some mix, and a small pitcher of vodka martinis. Carol settled herself comfortably in my armchair and watched me closely.

I returned the compliment. Her sheath had a Hong Kong-style slit up the side, and I could see plenty of flawless, tapering leg and even some smooth thigh.

I wondered what, if anything, she had on underneath the sheath. The way it fitted—smooth, without any underclothes marks showing—I was willing to bet there was nothing but Carol Champlain underneath.

The drinks arrived. We got to work on the first round to loosen the tensions.

Then she said, "I'm going to be straight with you, Vic. If you want to doublecross me, go ahead. You'll be signing my death warrant. But it wouldn't be smart. I happen to know that Klaus would like to rub you out just on general principles. You've got to watch your step with him. I get the idea you don't like him much. Eh?"

"He's not my most favorite person," I said.

"Nor mine. I hate his stinking guts."

"Huh? Why shack up with him if you hate him?"

"I don't have any choice," she said in a thin, bitter voice. "I can't leave him. He'd have me killed if I ever pulled out. He can't stand it when a girl walks out on him. I know he rubbed out the girl he had before me."

"Why do you stick with him?" I asked, pouring her a refill.

She shrugged, and the shrug did stunning things to the front of her sheath where the firm hills of her breasts pushed against the fabric. "I told you, I don't dare break loose. It's too risky."

"How'd you get mixed up with him in the first place?"

She said, "I got into trouble. Never mind what kind of trouble. Someone told Klaus about me and he got me out of the trouble. In return for which he expected certain favors. He took a fancy to me and one day he told me I was his Number One girl. That's how it happened."

My eyes narrowed. "So I can get into real big trouble if he finds out you're here. So what's on your mind?"

She said in a steady voice, "I've got a deal for you, Vic."

"Yeah?"

"I want you to kill Klaus for me."

"What's in it for me?"

"Two things," she said. "One is that you get me. The other is that I'll help you get the engraved plates for the

queer. We can head west together and set up in business
with those plates. You interested?"

"Maybe," I said. "If I'm sure you're not snowing me."

"I'm on the level," she said, and I believed her. "You
don't know how bad I want to get free of Klaus. And killing
him is the only way I can ever escape him." Her eyes glittered. "We'll work together. I know where the plates are.
We'll figure out some way of knocking Klaus off, and then
we'll grab the plates and get out of here. You won't regret
it, Vic. I can make a man happy."

"Can you?"

"You want me to prove it?"

"Wouldn't mind."

"Come here," she said.

She flowed out of the chair. I went to her, and her body
pressed up tight against mine, all those liquid curves tight
and soft against me. Our mouths met. Her kiss was fiery.

When we came up for air, she said, "Put your hand on
the back of my neck."

I did. There was a zipper there.

"Unzip me."

I unzipped her. The zipper ran from the nape of her
neck down to the beginning of her buttocks, and when I
finished unzipping she was halfway out of the sheath. She
stepped out of it and tossed it onto a chair.

I had been right. She had nothing on under it. Not a stitch.

I took a long look, and liked what I saw. High, firm breasts,
a flat belly, gorgeous legs. She was a girl who was made for
love. That was her role in life.

She came toward me, her lips parted, her eyes smoky. I opened my arms for her, and she glided right in, and we kissed again, longer than the first time. She was smiling at me, smiling with those bedroom eyes.

I let my hands rove over her body like I was handling precious jewels. Which I was, in a way. We eased over to the bed.

She said she was going to show me she could make a man happy.

She showed me.

She showed me for a couple of hours. By the time we were finished, I was very, very happy. So, I think, was she.

I was lying there in the dark puffing on a butt. It was about four in the morning or so. Carol was lying by my side. She had been asleep for a while. But suddenly she woke up.

"What time is it?"

I looked. "Quarter past four."

"I've got to be going."

"How come?"

"Klaus' goons may check my room in the morning. I wouldn't want them to tell Klaus I was somewhere else."

"Good point," I said.

She switched on a lamp and began to dress. I watched regretfully as she hid those supple curves from view, one at a time. Finally she was fully dressed and I had nothing but my imagination and my memories to tell me what those silken breasts and satiny thighs looked like and felt like. She said, "We all agreed, now?"

"I'm going to rub out Klaus. You're going to help me get the plates. Then we scram for the far west."

"Right."

"When?"

"Soon. I'll let you know. We've got to work things out so they mesh," she said. "Give me a couple of days to plan things."

"Sure," I said.

I went to the door with her. We had one last kiss. She was soft and warm and clinging, and I was sorry to see her go. Finally she left, and I went back to bed, feeling relaxed and easy about things. There are certain little rewards in this business, after all. Fringe benefits, you might say. I slept soundly.

SIX

Friday was half gone when I woke up. I was awakened by the sound of a ringing phone. I picked it up and heard Elena Szekely tell me she was downstairs and wanted to see me.

"I'll be right down," I told her. "Give me five minutes."

I shaved in a flash, dressed, and headed downstairs. She was in the lobby near the main desk. After the night with Carol, Elena looked more innocent, more virginal than ever. I said, "I haven't had breakfast yet. Want to join me in the coffee shop?"

We took a table. I ordered a healthy meal—Carol had left me with a ravenous appetite—and Elena ordered a glass of milk.

She said, "You have spoken to Klaus about my father?"

I shrugged. "I mentioned the matter to him."

"And?"

"He won't release him, Elena. Your father's much too valuable for him to let him go."

Tears glimmered in her eyes. "I knew it. I knew you could do nothing!"

"Hold on a sec," I said. "I never really thought I'd get anywhere talking to Klaus. But there are other ways of getting your father free."

"What?"

"Leave that to me," I said. "Just tell me where your father is kept. I'll arrange to get him out of there."

"You will not let him get hurt?"

"Don't worry. Everything will be fine."

She gave me the address. "But remember," she said. "Klaus will kill my father if he thinks anything is wrong. You must not tell the police."

"Don't worry about that," I assured her. "I don't tell the police anything, Elena. I'll get your father out of there my own way."

"I will be grateful. I will give anything to you. Anything. Only get him free!"

"Don't start that again, huh?"

"I mean it. I will be yours—if you will only free him!"

She left me soon afterward. And now I had a big asset— the whereabouts of the engraver. Maybe I couldn't get to him, but at least I knew where he was, and that was a big step in the right direction.

With Klaus out of town, there wasn't much I could do in the afternoon. I decided it might be an idea to go out to the address Elena had given me, and scout the place around. Get the feel of it.

I hailed a cab and gave him the address. "Whereabouts is that?" I asked

"North end of town."

I sat back and watched the meter click. Five bucks later, I said, "Let me know when you're a couple of blocks away."

"We're a couple of blocks away right now."

"Okay. Let me off right here."

I paid him and got out. He drove away, and I continued on foot. This was a sleepy, seedy section of Philly, with a lot of identical houses on every block. I crossed the street cautiously and scanned the numbers on the houses.

Old Szekely was being kept in Number 1132. I walked along the odd-number side of the street, looking.

And I saw.

I saw a house with its blinds drawn, and a big mobsterish-looking limousine parked in the driveway. It was 1132. It looked like a fortress, even though it was just a simple, shabby brick two-story house. She'd said he was held in a room upstairs, though he did his work for Klaus from a windowless room in the basement. That was also where they kept the plates, she'd told me.

There was a kid playing near the end of the block. I walked up to him and said, "How'd you like to make a quarter, kid?"

"How?" He looked sassy.

I pointed to 1132. "Go over there and ring the door-bell. Keep ringing it till somebody answers. When the door opens, ask them if they need their lawn mowed. Then leave."

"That's all?"

"That's all."

He looked at me like I was nuts. "Okay," he said. "Pay in advance."

I dug down, gave him a quarter. The kid—he was all of nine—crossed the street and started up the steps of 1132, while I faded back into an alleyway to watch.

He rang the bell. Nothing happened. He rang it again. The door opened about half an inch. I saw a nose stick suspiciously out. The kid talked to somebody for half a second, then turned and walked away.

They were taking no chances. I wondered how many goons were in there guarding the engraver. They had the place under guard, for sure. I couldn't just walk in there and yank Szekely out.

I faded away, crossed the street, headed back to the nearest big street, and got a cab.

"The Penn Plaza," I said.

Cracking into that place wouldn't be a cinch. But maybe I could get someone to do the job for me. Maybe.

It was time to phone Litwhiler, up in New York, and get him into the act.

I put through a long-distance call to the New York number he had given me, and asked for Harold as directed. There was some mumbo-jumbo at the other end, but finally Litwhiler's voice said, "Litwhiler here."

"Lowney."

"What's up?"

"Plenty," I said. "The wheels are turning. We're in business, Litwhiler."

"Tell me more, man."

I wet my lips. "Item number one," I said, "I know where the engraver is. And the plates. Item number two, I can get him for you. Item number three, I'm *willing* to get him for you."

"Item number four," Litwhiler said, "you've got yourself a deal. I mentioned a figure the other day. Is it okay?"

"Twenty-five grand to me, right?"

"Right."

"It's a deal," I said.

"Okay. When does all this happen?"

"Anytime you want," I said. "Just let me know how you want to arrange it."

"This weekend?"

"Why not," I said.

"Give me a day or so to get my end of it organized," he said. "Will you need men?"

"I guess I will," I told him. "Look, I'll call you tomorrow when things are in clearer shape. Meantime you round up your squad. I'll be in touch."

"Yeah," he said. "I'll be looking to hear from you."

I put down the phone. So much for Litwhiler.

Things were moving right along.

SEVEN

That night I called Klaus, figuring I'd up my bid a little if he had come back from his out-of-town trip. But Klaus wasn't there. I talked to Minton instead.

The snotty secretary said, "He won't be in till later tonight, Lowney."

"What time later?"

"How should I know? Nine, ten."

"Okay. I'll call him then. I'm going out for some dinner now. Tell him I've been calling."

"I'll think about it," he said.

"Listen, you stupid punk, you've got some lessons in manners coming to you. And maybe the next time I see you I'll take care of giving them to you."

I slammed down the phone. Feeling tense and hot under the collar, I went downstairs, ordered a cab, and told the driver to take me to the best restaurant in town. If I had to waste time, I thought, I was going to do it in style, and let the expense account boys sweat over my vouchers.

He took me to a French restaurant a block or two south of City Hall, which was a distance I could have walked for myself if I felt like it. The restaurant had no tables, they told me, but a discreet fiver slipped to the maître d' changed that situation in a hurry. I was taken to a table on the upper level of the restaurant.

Plush was the word for it. Red velvet on the walls,

mirrors everywhere, enough waiters and busboys to fill Yankee Stadium down to the last seat.

I had no complaints about the meal. Oysters and Chablis, vichyssoise, Scotch grouse accompanied by Mouton Rothschild '52—no, not a bad little meal at all, even if it did set my expense account back to the tune of $31.50, including tip and the two snifters of VSOP cognac that I helped wash my coffee down with.

It was a fine night, crisp and clear and fresh, so I decided to walk back to the Penn Plaza and use up some of the calories I had just consumed.

That was a mistake.

It could almost have been a fatal mistake.

I was sauntering along Market Street in a leisurely way when I passed a narrow alleyway, about three blocks from the hotel. I had just half a second to see some shadowy figures lurking in the alleyway. Then they leaped at me.

I sidestepped one, but two others dragged me into the alley.

It was dark in there. I couldn't see faces. I could see shapes, though, and I swung out hard, landing a couple of solid punches in someone's belly. I heard a hoodlum vomiting.

Then I heard the click of a safety being removed.

I flattened myself against the wall. There was the sudden roar of a gun and a bullet whizzed past my face. The flash gave me enough light to see by, and by then I had my own .38 out. I answered the fire, and someone yelped and grunted in pain.

Then I heard footsteps. Running away.

I struck a match. The alley was empty. The idiots had scrammed.

Not a very well-organized assassination party, I had to admit. What the hell, though. They had come close, and if they had had any brains I'd have been a dead man now. I felt that $31.50 dinner starting to turn a little sour around the edges inside me. Staring death in the face isn't good for the digestion.

I hurried back to the hotel before my playmates, whoever they were, came back for a second try.

My phone was ringing as I let myself into my room. I snatched it up.

"Hello?"

"Vic? Carol here." She was breathing fast. "I can't talk long. Listen, Vic, Minton sent some goons out to rub you out tonight. You've got to be careful. You—"

"It's too late, Carol. I've already met them."

"Are you all right?"

"Just a little winded. They weren't very smart goons. I shot one of them."

"Oh, I'm so glad! I was terrified they'd get you—I've been trying to call all evening. Ever since I overheard them planning it."

"Doesn't Klaus object when his little man goes around eradicating business associates? Or did Klaus put him up to it?"

"No, this was strictly Minton's idea. He figured he'd knock you off while Klaus was out of town."

"He isn't back yet?"

"No. He ought to be, any minute. I hear talk that they're trying to cut you and Hammell out of the deal, though. That he's negotiating with someone else."

"Huh?"

"That's all I know. I can't talk any more now. Be careful, Vic. They're all out to get you here. Don't take any chances. Remember our deal."

"Sure thing."

She blew me a kiss. I returned it.

She hung up.

So Minton had been behind that crude rubout attempt, eh? Just a little matter of personal pique, I guessed. I had humiliated him, and so he was trying to take care of me. But not trying very well.

I decided to turn the screw on him a little. I called Klaus' number, and got Minton again.

"Lowney?" He sounded surprised to hear from me alive.

"None other," I said. "Klaus back yet?"

"Not yet. You gonna keep bugging me all night?"

"I enjoy it, sonny-boy." I let the phone drop into its cradle.

I called back three more times that evening. The first two, I was told that Klaus had not yet come back. The third time, which was around midnight, the word was that Klaus was back, but had gone to bed. The word "bed" was delivered with such a lip-smacking leer that I had a vivid picture of Carol Champlain naked in Klaus' bedroom, with the crime czar greedily caressing the soft curving goodies and asking her if she'd been a good girl while he was away.

"You can reach him after noon tomorrow," I was told.

I called Klaus again at five after twelve Saturday morning. This time I got through to him.

"I hear you've been trying to get me," he said. "Sorry but I was out of town."

"So I hear."

"What's on your mind, Lowney?"

"First thing is just to tell you that I got shot at last night. You know, that's no way to treat a visitor from out of town, Klaus. Hammell wouldn't like it if his man came home to L.A. on a slab."

"I don't know anything about this, Lowney."

"Well, maybe somebody in your organization does. Anyway, I think you ought to check, just in case those boys happened to be in your outfit. Because they did such a lousy bungling job that they deserve to be fired."

"I tell you it wasn't our bunch, Lowney. Maybe some other outfit is after your skin. Not us."

I let that pass. "The other thing is, I've talked to Hammell and I've been given permission to raise my bid a little. But this is final. We'll offer—"

"Hold it," he said.

"What's the matter?"

"Save the bid for tonight. Come over here around eight-thirty, nine o'clock tonight and we can have a little auction. There's another bidder involved now."

"Huh?"

"I didn't like the way you were bidding," Klaus said evenly. "So I got in touch with another boy from out your way. Ricky Chavez. He'll be coming in by jet this afternoon, and he'll be over at my place tonight. You'll like to see your old pal again, I imagine. And the two of you can bid against each other for my merchandise."

The phone went dead.

My jaw dropped. My flesh crawled a little.

Ricky Chavez coming to town? Meeting me face to face?

That was a catastrophe. Chavez, I knew, had once been part of Hammell's organization. But he had split away, three or four years ago, to form his own rival bunch. He generally covered the territory south of L.A., down to San Diego. He was a thorn in Charley Hammell's side.

I didn't like the idea of having another bidder in town. That confused the situation, blurred things.

But much worse than that was the thought that the guy who was coming in was Ricky Chavez.

Chavez knew what the real Vic Lowney looked like.

Chavez would spot me for a phony the minute he laid eyes on me.

And there was no way I could get out of the meeting at Klaus' tonight. I had to go. And when I walked in and Klaus introduced me to Chavez as "Vic Lowney," there was going to be all hell to pay. Maybe.

I was going to have to play this situation by ear. But I had to risk it. Even though there was a fifty-fifty chance that the undertaker would be fitting me with a shroud before the night was over.

EIGHT

At half past eight I arrived at Klaus' suite at the Burke. Klaus was long past the stage of sending chauffeurs to transport me; I took a cab.

One of the goons answered the door. But it was Minton who came from within to greet me. He gave me a cold glare of pure hatred. I smiled warmly in return.

"Take me to your leader," I said lightly.

He muttered, "Lowney, one of these days—"

"Go on," I said. "One of these days *what*?" My fists opened and closed a couple of times, meaningfully.

Minton scowled. "Skip it. The boss is expecting you inside."

"Is he alone?"

"He's got company. Ricky Chavez is with him."

"That's nice," I said. "I haven't seen my old pal Ricky since he got out of reform school. Which way?"

"You know the way by now."

"Show me, pal. I'm a guest here."

Minton said something under his breath and led me through the suite to Klaus' office. He knocked, and Klaus said to come on in. Minton opened the door for me.

Klaus and Chavez were sitting at the table, both of them facing the door, with a big pile of probably phony bills in front of them. Klaus gave me a look of sullen dislike. The expression on Ricky Chavez' face was a totally blank one.

I strode forward, coming in on an angle to block my face from Klaus. I thrust my hand at Chavez and said heartily, "Hello there, Ricky-boy! How about a big handshake for your old buddy Vic Lowney?"

And I winked as hard as I knew how.

Chavez could have blown the whole thing up right then and there. All he needed to do was say, "Who the hell are *you*, buster?" But he didn't. He was smarter than that. He threw me a quick glance that said, *"You better be prepared to explain this deal later, Jack."* Then he stood up and extended his hand.

"Hello, Lowney," he said without enthusiasm.

"You boys sound like great pals," Klaus said.

"We are," I told him. "We were juvenile delinquents together. Then we grew up and became adult delinquents. How you been, Ricky?"

"No complaints," he said thinly. "How's the wife, Lowney?"

"You been reading the gossip columns? Last I heard I didn't have a wife."

"Just wondering," Chavez said. "Must have been some other guy I heard got married last month."

He gave me a sly look. I knew damned well Lowney didn't have any wives. Chavez was just trying to confuse me a little, to see how much I knew about Lowney, to find out just what in blazes I was up to. I favored him with a brotherly smile.

He was a dapper little fellow, no more than five feet six,

impeccably dressed. There was Latin American blood in him, and as so often happens he had a kind of hybrid attractiveness, with his dark glossy hair, even features, and smooth Latin look.

They said he was hell on wheels with women, and no wonder. But there was a steely glint in his eyes, and I knew he could handle himself with a gun. *Un hombre muy* tough, Chavez was. And knew it.

I decided on the informal approach.

"You have a good flight, Chavez?"

"Lousy. Storms all the way this side of the Rockies. How long you been here, Lowney?"

"Since Tuesday. The town's a drag."

"I hear you got shot at," he said.

"Only once. Dull town. Where'd you hear?"

"I told him," Klaus put in. "I thought he'd be amused."

I laughed. "Yeah. It was a riot." Without being asked, I pulled the decanter of Scotch across the table toward me and filled my glass, dumping a couple of cubes in from the ice-bucket.

Klaus wasn't minded to be very hospitable. I could tell that he and Chavez had already talked business, and if they hadn't agreed on terms they were probably pretty close. I was being frozen out, that was obvious. There was a definite sense of a link between them that didn't include me. I sipped my drink.

Chavez picked up a stack of paper money and fondled it. "They turn out a nice product here, eh, Lowney?"

"Passable."

"I'll say. They tell me you aren't willing to pay very much for it, though."

I shrugged. "I made what I considered was a fair offer."

"Mr. Klaus here didn't think so."

I said to Klaus, "Does this mean you two have already clinched a deal?"

Klaus gave me the Mona Lisa smile. "We've discussed some terms. There's no agreement yet."

"I'm still in the running, then?"

"The only one who's eliminating you is yourself, Lowney," Klaus said gently. "There was no real reason for me to call Chavez here in the first place. Except that you decided you wanted to bleed me."

The atmosphere in the room was getting frostier by the moment. And I was sitting with my back to the door, which I didn't care for at all. If Klaus had reached terms with Chavez, they might have decided to elect me odd man out. Unobtrusively I slipped out of my chair and began to wander around the room, taking care to keep myself close to the table. Any bullet aimed at me would have to pass through Klaus or Chavez first,

I said, "Okay, let's talk turkey. Tell me what your bid is, Chavez. If I can undercut it, I will. If I can't, I'll be on the next plane out of here."

Klaus said, "That isn't a businesslike way of doing things, Lowney."

"Why not?"

"This isn't exactly a public auction. I've got a better idea."

"Which is?"

"Written bids." He handed each of us a sheet of paper and an envelope. "Write down your best price and seal it in the envelope. I'll open them after you've gone and I'll notify the successful bidder. I might warn you, Lowney, that Chavez knows your bid and plans to raise it substantially, so if you want the contract you'd better be prepared to back down a ways."

I sat down again—at the side of the table, with my eyes on the door. Klaus was fidgeting. Shielding his paper, Chavez scribbled something quickly and put the paper in the envelope. Staring off into space, I tried hard to look like I was faced with a difficult decision.

After a long moment I uncapped the pen and wrote, *My best offer is eight cents on the dollar, pickup in Philly and transcontinental transport at our expense. Not a penny higher. Lowney.*

I sealed the envelope and handed it to Klaus. He put it in his desk without looking at it.

"All right," he said. "So much for business. You fellows in the mood for some cards?"

Chavez was. I went along.

Klaus pressed a buzzer and Carol entered, carrying a tray with some decks of cards and chips. She was wearing a blue cocktail dress that showed just about everything she had above the waist, and she took good care to bend way over when she put the cards down. When she had, she circled behind Klaus and Chavez and, facing me, silently shaped the word *Careful* with her lips, and rolled her eyes toward the door. Then she tiptoed out.

A three-man card game can be pretty dull unless it's for blood. This one was. After half an hour I found myself behind some four hundred bucks, and a little while later I was down a thousand and some. My luck started to change, and I began to catch up. Carol kept going in and out, filling our glasses, but I didn't drink much.

Klaus and Chavez were watching me closely. So far as I could tell the cards were straight and there was no collusion between the two of them. But I had the impression Klaus was waiting for a chance to catch me cheating and have me taken care of.

I didn't give him the opportunity. I played it straight and hard, wiggled out of the hole, and after a spell I was about even, with Chavez maybe fifty ahead and Klaus fifty behind. I tossed in my cards.

"I've had it," I said. "I think I'll take off."

"Stick round," said Klaus. "The evening's young."

"Not for me. I've had a busy day." I walked quickly toward the door and yanked it open.

One of Klaus' goons was standing there with a blank look of amazement on his face. I dragged him into the room. Turning to Klaus, I said, "What was this one doing there?"

"He's my bodyguard," Klaus said glibly. "Whenever I'm alone with strangers he's posted out there. He's a hundred percent trustworthy."

It wasn't a very probable story, but I couldn't argue with it. Whatever plans Klaus might have had for ambushing me this evening, they had evaporated with nothing coming of them.

I said, "Okay. Will you be in touch with me about the contract?"

"I'll let you know who had the high bid," Klaus said. "Don't call us. We'll call you."

"Any way you want. Goodnight, Klaus. See you back in L.A., Chavez."

"Hold on," Chavez said, getting up. "I think I'll be moving along too."

Klaus looked displeased. "Stick around a while, Ricky. It's early yet."

Chavez shook his head. "I'm not used to this time zone yet. I can use some sleep. Anyway, I want to have a little chat with my old buddy Vic here."

We walked out together—past the goons, past Minton, past Carol, past the whole organization with which Klaus had surrounded himself. While we waited for the elevator, Chavez said conversationally, "Where you staying?"

"The Penn Plaza. You?"

"The Bingham."

Minton appeared abruptly. He said, "Mr. Klaus says to wait a moment, he'll let you have a chauffeur to take you home."

"Never mind," Chavez said. "We'll take a cab."

"Suit yourself," Minton said, and went back inside. The elevator arrived. We got in and the door slid smoothly shut, as though flowing on oil.

Chavez leaned against the rail and said, "You were pretty smooth in there, man."

"Thanks. You were okay yourself, Chavez. You've got

good reactions. Anybody else might have given me away the second I walked through the door."

"How dumb do you think I am?"

"Not very. I think you're a hell of a shrewd cookie, Chavez. If you don't mind my saying so."

He seemed to lose interest in me. The elevator continued its long glide down from the penthouse, and Chavez took out what looked like a gold toothpick and set to work on his molars. The elevator arrived at the lobby. We strolled out, into the coolish night.

There was a cab waiting at a hack stand on the corner. I started to signal it, but Chavez caught my arm and dragged it down. "Don't."

"Why not?"

"I'm not ready to go home," he said. He pointed across the street, to a neon bar sign. "Let's go get a couple of drinks. I want to talk to you, man."

I didn't object. We crossed the street, but as we got to the bar the neon sign winked out.

"What the hell?" Chavez grunted.

"It's 12:01 Saturday night," I said. "Which means it's Sunday morning. Which means you can't legally buy a drink in Philadelphia."

Chavez delivered himself of two short, emphatic sentences that would have sizzled the ears of any loyal inhabitant of the City of Brotherly Love. Then he said, "We'll go to my place instead."

*

He didn't wait for my opinion. He waved for the cab I had tried to signal, and we got in. We rode to the Bingham in silence. It was an old-line hotel, well upholstered and conservative looking. We entered Chavez' sprawling suite on the eighth floor, and he locked and chained the door carefully.

Then he whirled around to face me. I had half a foot of height on him, but he glared up commandingly all the same.

"All right, buster," he said frigidly. "We both know you aren't Vic Lowney. I want to know who the hell you *are,* man."

NINE

I let him know I wasn't afraid of him. I strolled around him, lowered myself into an overstuffed armchair, and loosened my tie. Only then did I deign to answer.

"The name doesn't matter," I said. "Call me Joe if you have to."

"Cut the crap," he hissed. "What kind of caper are you pulling? Where's Lowney?"

"Dead," I said

He recoiled. "You're funning me, mister. I hate that. I ain't got any sense of humor along that line."

"I said Lowney is dead," I told him evenly. "He's resting in the dear old California sod, under eight feet of dirt in Jovenita Canyon. I put him there."

"Don't fun me, man," he said getting tense and looking menacingly at me. "It takes more than you got to plow Vic Lowney under."

"Suit yourself. Believe it or not."

"Wise guy."

"I cooled Lowney off. If you don't want to believe it, Chavez, you know what you can do about it."

His handsome face turned ugly all at once. The eyelids drooped, the lower lip curled up tight. I knew he had a gun somewhere under his jacket, and I knew Ricky Chavez had a low boiling point. Any second he'd go for the gun. Maybe not to shoot, just to pistol-whip me a little. I got ready.

"I don't like punks to talk to me that way," Chavez crooned. "For the last time, who the blazes are you and how'd you slip into this caper?"

"I killed Lowney and took his place on the plane."

"Goddamit, don't give me that crap! Lowney could cut down six of you!"

"You're wasting my time, Chavez, I give you answers and you don't listen to them." I started up out of the chair, ostensibly heading for the door. But Chavez reacted as I expected. The right hand went diving into the jacket to get the gun. I swung to my left and caught hold of him as though we were going to waltz, wrapping my left arm around his shoulders and grabbing his jacket-front with my right. He couldn't draw his gun out of the jacket—or his hand, for that matter. His face was white with hatred and surprise. I held him tight.

"Let go of the gun, Ricky."

"You son of a bitch—"

"Let go of it. You're only making trouble for yourself." He got so tensed up his arm started to shake. I guess nobody had ever handled him this way before. I cradled him tight, and after a moment I felt his right arm relax inside the jacket. I stepped away from him quickly, drawing my own gun and covering him.

Chavez looked like a trapped rat. "You stinking bastard," he murmured.

"Don't be rude, Ricky. I didn't ask you to go pulling on me. I came up here for a nice friendly chat."

"Put the gun away, man."

"I don't know if that would be smart."

"I won't draw on you," he whispered harshly.

I eyed him for a moment, then slid the gun back into its holster. Chavez licked his lips unhappily. His eyes were like little slits. But I knew I had him. It was the first time in his life he'd ever been boxed in, and he was afraid to start things a second time.

"*Now* do you believe I cooled off Vic Lowney?" I asked.

He sat down, looking a little limp. "Yeah," he said hoarsely. "Yeah. Sure. Imagine that. Does Hammell know about it?"

"Not yet. He thinks Lowney's in Philadelphia."

"And you been fooling Klaus all this time?"

"Yep."

Chavez shook his head "What's the pitch, man?"

"I'm out for me, is all."

"Who the crap are you, anyway?"

I shrugged. "Call me Joe, if you want, like I said. I'm from Vegas."

"I never seen you there."

"You never looked. I've got a stake in the Côte d'Azur, on the Strip. I spend most of my time in Mexico, though. Acapulco."

"How'd you get into the Lowney caper?"

I took a fastidious look at my fingernails before answering. "I got friends. They told me about the kind of queer Klaus was printing. They told me Vic Lowney was going to Philly to tie up the California distributorship for Hammell. I'm around Lowney's size and build. I know a lot about him. And I owed him something, anyway. Sort of killing two birds with one stone."

"You cooled him off?" Chavez said. He still didn't believe it.

I nodded. "I went out to Pacific Palisades Monday night and rang the doorbell at two in the morning. Lowney came to the door himself and I shot him. Just as simple as that. Dumped him in the car, drove him up to the canyon country, buried him. The next morning I got on the plane and came right here."

"Klaus didn't suspect?"

"Klaus never met Lowney. I had everything all sewed up, I thought. Only you had to bust in."

Chavez grinned faintly. "Klaus told me you offered him a nickel on the dollar. You didn't seriously figure to make a deal like that, man?"

"It couldn't hurt to start low. I could always up the ante later, I figured. I didn't figure Klaus would bring *you* into the picture."

"Sometimes you can't figure everything, man." Chavez was warming to me, now. To salvage his own pride at being pushed around the way I had pushed him around, he had to build me up in his own mind as somebody special, somebody worth knowing. He leaned forward and flashed a smile. "I like you, man. You've got guts. And you did me a big favor, too."

"What kind of favor?"

"Cutting Hammell out of this deal. You know how I feel about Hammell? I feel like I want to cut his face off with a razor. That's how much I hate that bastard. And you just sideswiped him out of the whole Klaus deal for me. He'll pop his cork when he finds out that I'm handling the Klaus product on the Coast."

"You're overlooking one thing, Chavez."

"Which is?"

"That I'm still in the picture. Maybe Hammell isn't, but *I* am."

"The hell you are. You don't seriously think you'll get the contract at your price?"

I smiled evenly. "My price can be raised. I can match everything you put up, plus. That's what I told Klaus in the bid. I offered him two cents per dollar higher than your bid, whatever your bid was."

"If you're joking me—"

"I'm dead serious," I said. "Klaus won't risk swindling me. I said the deal was contingent on his showing me your bid. So he'll call me tomorrow and say the contract's mine."

Chavez' face grew cloudy again. He made a snarling incoherent sound.

I said, "What was your bid, Chavez?"

"Twenty cents on the dollar."

"So I get it for twenty-two," I mused. "More than I wanted to put up, but less than Klaus was asking. And the product is damned good."

Chavez was building up toward the boiling point again.

I could practically see the dials spinning round, getting closer and closer to *overload.*

He said in a hollow voice, "You ain't got the organization to handle it right."

"How do you know?"

That stymied him, but only for a moment. "I know because there ain't no gangs I don't know about. You're a lone wolf, aren't you?"

"Like hell. I've got men. We'll operate out of Vegas, spreading the stuff there and in Cal. And across the border too. A Mex isn't so fussy about the printing on his bills as long as they say United States of America on them."

"Damn you, I'll call Klaus and offer twenty-three!" Chavez muttered.

"My bid stands. Two cents per hundred above anything you offer."

"Anything? Suppose I offer ninety-eight?"

I laughed. "I'll let you have it, man. I give you a tip: I drop out of the bidding above fifty cents on the dollar. So that's what you can shoot for."

"It isn't worth it," he grumbled. His fingers started to get itchy, as though he were beginning to decide that it would be a lot cheaper to eliminate me right here and now. I smiled and pointed at his middle.

"Don't get ideas about the gun, Chavez. You'll lose again, and you'll lose hard the second time."

He scowled at me. "I'll get you. Maybe not now, but later. You ain't gonna take this deal away from me. I promise you that, man."

"You've got the wrong approach, Chavez. I'm not looking for any trouble."

"You're gonna get it, though!"

"Ease up, man. Let me say my say. There's no reason why we've got to threaten each other. We can go into partnership instead."

He looked at me as if I'd just said something in Sanskrit. *"Partnership?"* he repeated incredulously.

"Sure. Why let Klaus bulldoze us? I'll call him tomorrow and tell him I'm withdrawing my bid. You get the contract by default, at twenty cents per hundred. Maybe you can even sweat him down to sixteen or seventeen, being as you have the field to yourself."

He frowned suspiciously. "And then what? What's in it for you?"

"A cut," I said. "Three cents on every dollar goes to me."

"That's a pretty fat cut, man."

"It's better than fighting. The other way, either I get the contract at twenty-two, or you have to bid me all the way up to fifty to snag it for yourself. It's a lot cheaper to pay sixteen or seventeen to Klaus and three to me. And I'll cooperate on the Nevada distribution. Maybe I'll even let you use my men. We can—merge, Chavez. How about that? Instead of cutting each other's throats, we can team up and cut Hammell's throat instead."

"How do I know you ain't cruddin' me?"

"What's in it for me? I'd rather work with you than against you, Chavez. I like your style. And I got plenty of reasons for wanting to see Charley Hammell knocked off his high horse. With Lowney gone, it wouldn't be very hard to finish Hammell. Then you'd have the whole southwest tied up exclusive, Chavez. Isn't that better than wrangling with me?"

He smiled, slowly, grudgingly. "Yeah," he whispered finally. "Yeah."

"It's a deal, then?"

"Y-yeah." Hesitantly.

I stood up and gave him my hand. He got up reluctantly and we shook. It wasn't exactly a handshake between two men who trusted each other. But that was okay. I didn't need Chavez to trust me. Matter of fact, the best thing in the world that he could do was to doublecross me, which he probably would.

"I'll phone Klaus tomorrow and tell him my bid's cancelled. Then you can sweat the contract out of him on your own."

"Yeah."

"I'll be in touch with you on the Coast," I said. "I've got some business to tidy up in Vegas, and then I'll come to L.A. and we can get things all worked out. I'll be staying at the Beverly Wilshire, and you can reach me there after next week."

"Sure," Chavez said. There was a cold glitter in his eyes that he wasn't bothering to hide. "I'm glad we didn't have to fight. What's your last name, Joe?"

"Manners," I improvised.

"Joe Manners," he repeated. "Okay, Joe. I don't know you from Adam, but you handle yourself okay. I was just letting you push me around before, you know. Sort of like a test to see how good you really were."

"Sure, Ricky. I understand."

Our eyes met, and I made sure *he* understood. Little men often talk big in retrospect. By the time morning came around, Chavez would have convinced himself that he really had been only shamming when I blocked him from drawing his gun. These sawed-off killers live in little fantasy worlds where they're really six feet five and everybody bows to them.

I walked to the door.

"So long—partner."

"Yeah," Chavez said, deep in his throat. "So long, partner."

I closed the door behind me and rang for the elevator.

So I was Ricky Chavez' partner now. And I was in for a slice of his profits on the Klaus deal.

At least, that was the way it worked theoretically. But I knew what was on Chavez' mind. He was in a sweat to sign the contract with Klaus, so he was willing to agree to anything. The important thing was horning Hammell aside. He could always deal with a Joe Manners later.

Joe Manners wouldn't be getting any slices from Ricky Chavez. If Chavez had his way, the only thing Manners would end up by getting would be some lead in the belly.

TEN

I woke up early on Sunday morning. It was a bright, sunny day. The hotel coffee shop was a ghost town when I came in for breakfast, a little after nine. Philadelphia at nine o'clock on a Sunday morning is just one big morgue. The corpses don't start stirring until ten or eleven.

I didn't want to disturb the slumbers of my buddy Klaus, so I waited until half past eleven to phone him. The phone rang close to a dozen times, and just as I was about to give up I heard a click and then the extremely sleepy-sounding voice of Carol Champlain.

"Hello?"

"Morning, sweetheart. I wake you up?"

"Who's this?" She was still foggy.

"The name is Lowney. Perhaps you've heard of me. I come from California."

"Oh—oh, gosh. Vic. Hold on a second and let me get my eyes open."

"Must have been a big night, eh?"

She yawned. "Klaus had a celebration after you left. Champagne and everything. We didn't get to bed till almost five. Klaus is still asleep. Everybody else is gone."

"Just you and Klaus there?"

"And the bodyguards. They aren't supposed to answer the phone."

"Why the wing-ding?" I asked.

"Because of the deal," Carol said. "Vic, he's going to make a deal with that horrible little Chavez man."

"Did he say so?"

"No, he didn't say a thing. Except once or twice he remarked that he'd be glad to see you clear out. He hates you something fierce, Vic."

"I imagine he does. Let me talk to him, will you, honey?"

"He's asleep, Vic."

"Then wake him up."

"But—"

"Come on, Carol. I don't have all day to stand around waiting on Klaus. Roust him up."

"If you insist. But he's going to be sore as hell."

"I'll worry about that," I said. "You just get him out of bed."

A couple of minutes went by, and then Klaus came to the phone. He sounded surly, and his voice was an octave deeper than normal.

"Yeah?"

"Good morning, Klaus. You shouldn't sleep so late. You're missing all the sunshine."

"You got a hell of a nerve, Lowney. I feel like sending my guys out to rough you up and knock some manners into you. What the hell kind of hour is this to call on a Sunday morning?" he grumbled.

"Cool it, Klaus. I've got something on my mind."

"Yeah?"

"I just wanted to tell you that I'm withdrawing my bid.

Hammell wired me and told me not to make any deals with you. So it's all off."

"Isn't that nice?" Klaus growled. "Well, you could have saved yourself a phone call. And some breath. There isn't any need for you to withdraw your bid. Chavez outbid you by exactly twenty-five percent. I was going to call you both later and let you know."

"He gets the contract, right?"

"Right. So you don't have to bother me anymore, Lowney. You hear that?"

"I'm not deaf."

"You got your plane ticket back to L.A.?"

"You in a hurry to see me leave?"

"The quicker the better," Klaus said.

"Sorry to disappoint you. I'll be around town for another couple of days. Sightseeing."

"Just keep away from me,"

"You're one sight I've already seen. So long, Klaus. It was fun doing business with you. Congratulate Chavez for me. I guess the biggest sucker won."

I hung up, cutting off Klaus' angry sputter.

Now I had to wait. I had to give Chavez time to do my work for me.

I sat down on the edge of my bed and puffed on a cigarette, staring at the floor and trying to fit all the pieces of the jigsaw together. The way you work in this kind of operation, you've got to set up a smooth hunk of machinery that will weave and spin and finally clamp an unbreakable web around everyone you're trying to nail.

The only difficulty is that the parts of the machine are of necessity human beings. And you can set human beings in motion, but you can't always control the direction they move in....

After a while you get to be a pretty fair psychologist. You size up your people and you decide what stimulus A will produce effect B. And if you're lucky, it happens that way. If you aren't, they bury you.

The X in my equation now was Chavez. And that goes to show you: Chavez hadn't been on the scene at the start, hadn't even figured into my original hazy size-up of the situation. Neither had Litwhiler. You have to be prepared for new developments. You have to know how to turn them to your own advantage.

The hours slid by. The pile of cigarette butts in the ashtray grew top-heavy.

I started phoning Chavez at half past one. I got no answer. I called every fifteen minutes, until the Bingham switchboard girl got to recognizing my voice, and every time I asked for Chavez she said sweetly, "I don't believe he's back yet, but I'll ring his suite for you, sir," and then she rang, and then she chirped, "I'm terribly sorry, sir, but Mr. Chavez still does not answer. Shall I take a message for you?"

"No thanks. I'll keep trying."

I did. I hung on the phone for two hours, ringing every fifteen minutes. I don't know how that Bingham switchboard girl kept her patience.

And then, at quarter to four, I was reaching wearily for

the telephone again when it began to ring of its own accord. I picked up. "Hello?"

"Vic? Carol here." She sounded breathless. "I'm calling from a payphone in the lobby of the Burke. I can't talk long. Klaus thinks I went down to buy some candy bars. Vic, there isn't any time left. They're going to kill you!"

"They tried it once and it didn't work."

"No, not Minton this time. Klaus and Chavez."

"What?"

"Chavez was here all afternoon. I heard them talking. Vic, are you—are you *really* Vic Lowney?"

"Why?" I asked.

"Chavez said you weren't. He said you were somebody named Manners, from Las Vegas, and that you had—killed Lowney and were impersonating him. Is that true?"

"It might be," I said tightly.

"Well, Chavez suggested to Klaus that they get rid of you. As long as they don't have to worry about the Hammell organization avenging you, Chavez said, it was the smart thing to do. And Klaus agreed. So they're going to get you before you leave Philadelphia. Vic, is it true—what Chavez said?"

"It's true," I told her. "I'm not Lowney. I'm an independent. A lone wolf. Chavez is afraid I'm going to cut in on him."

"I'm all mixed up. Vic—Joe—"

"Did they say when they were going to jump me?"

"Tomorrow, I think. Or maybe even tonight if they can work it. Listen, darling, we've got to move fast. You remember what we talked about before? Killing Klaus and going west together?"

"Are you still with me?" I asked. "Now that you know I'm not Lowney?"

"Of course. It's *you* I want—whoever you are."

I didn't stop to ponder the philosophical implications of that statement. I said, "Okay. How are we going to work it?"

"Klaus has a roadhouse just outside of Philly," Carol said. "It's on Route One down near Lansdowne. Restaurant and a bar, and dancing Saturday nights, and rooms for rent upstairs. It's closed today. I've got a spare key, though. I stole it from Klaus a long time ago and he's never missed it."

"Go on."

"I'll meet you now and give you the key. You go down there, let yourself in, and wait. Then I'll get Klaus in a frisky mood and make him take me for a drive."

"Are you sure you can?" I asked.

"I was very nice to him last night. *Very* nice," she said bitterly. "And he's in a good mood now, on account of tying up with Chavez. Don't worry—I'll twist his arm a little. I'll make him drive me south on Route One, and when we pass the roadhouse I'll suggest that we get out and use one of the bedrooms for a while. Klaus will be agreeable.

"The moment he steps out of the car, *bang*, you shoot him from one of the upstairs windows. When the chauffeur gets out, you shoot him too. It's deserted down there; nobody will hear anything much. Then we get into the car and drive back to town. We grab Szekely and the plates, and head for the Coast."

"You've got everything figured out nice and neat," I said.

"I have a lot of spare time to think about things."

"Where can we meet for the key?"

"The north side of City Hall. In forty-five minutes I'll hand you the key and you get down to the roadhouse by seven-thirty or so."

"Right."

"And—be careful, Vic—Joe—whoever. Klaus' men may be out looking for you already. Klaus wants to kill you real bad, now that he knows you aren't Lowney after all."

I promised I'd take care of myself, and told Carol I'd be at City Hall at four-thirty sharp.

Hanging up, I stubbed out my cigarette and walked to the window. I was in a spot now.

Chavez ratting to Klaus, that was okay. I had wanted him to do just that and he had cooperated. But this other business, of knocking off Klaus at a roadhouse outside town, that wasn't in my scheme of things at all.

It was handy to know about the roadhouse, handier to have the key. But I wasn't eager to do a hatchet-job on Klaus. Leave that sort of stuff for the judges and juries. My job is just to get them behind bars.

On the other hand, if I failed to eradicate Klaus, if I backed down in any way, I'd lose Carol's sympathy and possibly even arouse her suspicions. And Carol was a valuable ally. She was my one reliable pipeline out of Klaus' organization.

I stewed over the problem for a while, trying to figure out some way I could keep Carol interested in me and simultaneously not have to shoot Klaus. I didn't have any easy answers to that one. Carol had been very useful to me, but now her enthusiasm was fouling things up, as she tried to collect on the promissory note I had given her in the matter of knocking off Klaus and carrying her off to the sunny southwest.

One thing I hate is stepping into a situation without knowing which way I'm heading. I don't like to play by ear. But I had no choice now. I would just have to go along from one minute to the next, and trust to luck.

At quarter after four I left my room and went downstairs. I stepped warily out of the hotel, looking in all directions. For all I knew, Klaus' murder squadron was squatting right across the street, waiting to blow my head off the moment I set foot outside the Penn Plaza. But nothing happened. I pulled my coat collar up around my ears and started walking east along Market toward the big hunk of masonry that is Philadelphia's City Hall.

It was growing dark already, and a chill wind was blowing. I picked my way through the heavy Sunday afternoon traffic circling round City Hall, crossed the plaza and took up a station at the north end, just under the arch. It was half past four. No sign of Carol. I lit up a cig and waited.

Five minutes later, a taxicab pulled up about a hundred feet away, and a tall girl in a mink got out and started running toward the arch.

She never got there.

The instant the taxi pulled away, a long black sedan glided into the spot vacated. A window rolled down and a hand came out. A hand holding a gun.

"Carol!" I yelled.

She didn't stop. She was too busy running toward me, grinning and waving. I saw Minton's face peering out that car window, taking dead aim.

He fired.

The shot smashed into Carol from behind and knocked her down. He fired a second time, as she fell, but the slug glanced off the pavement. Catching sight of me, he pumped two quick bullets my way. I hit the sidewalk fast and heard the echoes of the shots go shuddering past me through the arch. Then the traffic light changed, and the sedan sped away.

I sprinted to Carol.

ELEVEN

She was lying on her side, in a twisted position, and the blood was soaking right through the mink and forming a little puddle on the sidewalk. I knelt by her side. Her eyes were glazing fast, and her face, drained of blood, looked ghostly. She looked up at me, her head lolling, and tried to say something. "Minton…never trusted me… always jealous. Tapped…phone…they knew I was seeing you…. Vic…."

She sank back. I threw open her coat and saw that there wasn't much use calling an ambulance. One shot had been enough. For once Minton hadn't bungled. He had used a .45, and the big slug had entered right between her shoulder blades, bored through her body at tremendous force, and had emerged smack between her lovely breasts, half an inch to the right of the sternum.

There was a hole in her blouse with the diameter of a half dollar, and that hole went right through her body, heart and all. She had stayed alive for thirty seconds after the shot on sheer willpower, nothing more.

The key, I thought.

As I half expected, she was clutching it in her hand. The fingers hadn't started to get stiff yet, of course, but her grip was tight. I pried the key loose and slipped it into my pocket, and not a moment too soon, either, because the next minute the place was full of cops.

I got to my feet. Two of the cops bent to examine Carol, a third went running off to call an ambulance, and a fourth pointed to me.

"What happened here?"

I shrugged. "The girl got out of a cab. Another car pulled up and somebody shot her. They fired four shots altogether and drove away."

"Which way?"

"Around the building. How should I know?"

"What were you doing here?" he snapped.

"Just looking around," I said. "I'm from out of town. This the way it always is in Philly on a Sunday afternoon? Seemed more like Chicago just now."

He had his notebook out and wasn't smiling. The cops examining Carol had decided by this time that she was dead, which didn't take any great powers of observation. Sherlock said, "Let's have your name."

"Wait a second, officer. That girl was shot from behind and I was in front of her. If you think—"

"You're a *witness*, Mack, not a suspect," he said with irritation. "In fact, you're just about the only good witness there was. What's your name?"

"Vic Lowney."

It didn't register on him. Evidently he wasn't up to date on the big names of California crime. "Where are you from?"

"Los Angeles."

"Local address?"

"I'm staying at the Penn Plaza."

"You know the girl at all?"

I shrugged. "I was just standing here, officer, and she got out of a cab. That's all I know."

I heard the wailing of an ambulance, and a moment later it pulled up at the curb. The stretcher crew came barreling out, but they could see right away that they weren't needed. The only place that girl was going was to the morgue.

My man wouldn't let up. "You say there were *four* shots?" he continued.

"That's what I said, yes."

"Only one wound on the body," he said. He turned to the other cops and set them looking around under the arch for the slugs. It didn't take long for them to find all four, including the one that had ripped the life out of Carol Champlain.

For a moment I thought they were going to take me down to headquarters. That would have been a nuisance; they might have asked questions, demanded identification, and generally made trouble for me—even jugged me overnight, which would have been very very awkward. In that case a phone call to Washington would clear things up. But I didn't want to tip my hand to the locals about being an undercover agent. I preferred to do my work without any well-meant assistance of that sort.

The policeman, though, was satisfied that I was just an innocent bystander who had happened to see the murder.

Telling me to stand by and remain available for an inquest, he let me go—warning me to notify the police if I checked out of the Penn Plaza.

It was only a couple of blocks back to the hotel, but I got a lift in the police car. I didn't mind that at all. Klaus' men had succeeded in eliminating Carol, but they were still hot to plow me under. And you can't always count on being able to duck in time.

I paced around my room for a while, using up half a pack of cigs in the process. Things were coming to a head, now. I didn't have much time left. Maybe twenty-four hours at the most to wrap everything up.

I felt sorry for Carol, the poor dumb hotpants. Not that she deserved any pity. In her world it's dog eat dog, and her tragedy was simply that she didn't get to Klaus before Klaus had gotten to her. But I missed her all the same. She had fed me a lot of helpful information, and she had made Thursday night bright and warm and cozy for me.

I told myself she was better off where she was. She had had it good for twenty-five or thirty years, and now she didn't have to worry about losing her figure, sprouting wrinkles, and ending up on the scrapheap.

She was there already. The fast way.

It was half past five before I had everything worked out. I checked it backwards and forwards, looking for weak spots. There were plenty of them. Even after long figuring, I couldn't eliminate them all. But I had a fifty-fifty chance, I figured, of making everything work out the way I wanted it to. An even break is all I ever ask.

Given that, I can usually bend the odds in my direction.

I picked up the phone. Litwhiler had given me a home telephone number, to use on Sunday if I had to, and I used it. I gave it to the operator and told her to make it person to person.

There was the usual Alphonse-and-Gaston routine with the operators. And then finally I was connected to Litwhiler.

"I've been waiting to hear from you all day, Lowney," he said. "What's holding things up?"

"Nothing, anymore. We're ready to roll."

"About time," he said. "Go on, fill me in."

I ran a hand through my hair, took a deep breath, and said, "The engraver is being kept in a roadhouse on Route One, south of Philly. Klaus owns the place. Dining and dancing downstairs, rooms for rent upstairs. They keep him in one of the rooms, under round-the-clock guard."

"Okay. Go on."

"The place closes around three in the morning," I said. "At half past three ayem, you and your boys come busting in. There are only a couple of guards, and you can take them easy."

"You're sure they won't hurt the old man any?" Litwhiler said uneasily. "I mean, if we come smashing in there, maybe they'll kill the engraver. Then it won't be worth our while."

"Don't worry about that," I assured him. "Klaus doesn't think that way. Anyhow, they won't be expecting trouble. The roadhouse is way out in the sticks, and nobody knows the old man lives there. You can just march in and take the place over. I've got the key to the front door."

"How'd you work that?"

"I lifted it from Klaus. He doesn't know. So you can meet me and I'll let you have the key. The rest ought to be child's play, Litwhiler."

He was silent a moment, thinking it over. Then he said at length, "Okay. I'll come down tomorrow night. How long does it take to reach this place from downtown Philadelphia?"

"Forty minutes," I said, guessing.

"Okay. We'll stop off at the Penn Plaza around quarter to three in the morning and get the key from you."

"And don't forget the twenty-five grand."

"You get that when the engraver's in our hands," Litwhiler said. "Say, do they keep the plates out at this place too?"

"The whole *megilla*," I said. "Plates, press, engraver, everything. There's a regular printing plant in the basement. You'll really have it made, Litwhiler."

"Great," Litwhiler said. "If everything works out right, I'll make this worth your while, Lowney. I never forget a man who helps me. I mean that."

He sounded so maudlin that it hurt. He went on in the same vein for another minute or so—piling it up on *my* phone bill—and then I got rid of him. Quarter to three, Tuesday morning, he and his bunch would be down to get the old man out of the roadhouse.

Of course, the old man wasn't *in* the roadhouse. But Litwhiler didn't need to know that.

I pondered things for a little while, and then started feeling hungry. I put away a good meal in the third-floor chophouse. My expense account on this caper was going to be a beaut. If I survived to submit a swindle sheet, that was.

After dinner, I checked my ammunition, changed my coat, and headed out again. Half the pincers had been forged, now—Litwhiler's half. Klaus would supply the other half and Chavez would be the bolt to hold the whole thing together. And once all was assembled, I just had to grab the handles and close everything nice and tight.

Except that there was a fly in the ointment, and a big one. The hitch was Elena Szekely. I needed to contact her, but I had no way of doing it. All the other times, she had come to *me*. I didn't dare phone her at home, with Klaus' goons all over the place, and I didn't know where else to reach her. So unless she contacted me some time in the next twenty-four hours, I'd be unable to communicate my plan to her, and things would be tougher than otherwise. She would be a floating variable in my equation. Well, it couldn't be helped.

I had to see Chavez first. And without making any appointments in advance.

I phoned the Bingham and said to the switchboard girl, "Is Mr. Chavez in?"

"I'll ring his room for you, sir."

On the second ring, Chavez picked up. He said hello, and the voice was unmistakably his. I hung up without saying a word, and went down to the Penn Plaza lobby. The bellhops bristled expectantly—they had learned that

Vic Lowney meant lots of easy tips to them—and I called one over. Dropping some change into his eager little palm, I said, "Get me a taxi, boy. Have him pull up right outside the hotel."

"Yes, Mr. Lowney," he said briskly, and off he went.

A moment later the cab was there. The doorman of the hotel held the cab door for me, and I scuttled quickly out and across the fifteen feet or so to the curb, and into the cab. I managed it so fast that any lurking Klaus assassins wouldn't have time to take aim.

Slouching down low in the back of the cab, I said, "Take me to the Bingham, driver."

The cab started off, down Market and around City Hall. I had an uncomfortable itchy feeling on the back of my neck, the sort of feeling you're very likely to get when you know that a bunch of .45-toting goons are camping around your hotel waiting for a chance to nail you.

The Bingham is about a fifteen-minute ride from the Penn Plaza. We were about five blocks away when I looked quickly out the rear window and saw the sedan following us. I didn't need to see the driver's face to know that this was the kill-car.

I cleared my throat and said, "When you reach the Bingham, driver, take me around to the side entrance. You know which I mean?"

"Yes, sir."

We went along for another couple of blocks. I didn't stick my head up high enough to see if the sedan was still behind us. The driver turned off Broad Street and started going around the Bingham to the back entrance, down one of those narrow little Philadelphia side streets, when all of a sudden the sedan leaped into view, darting ahead of us like a plunging shark.

The cab driver yelled. The sedan sideswiped us beautifully, and the cab plowed into somebody's Chrysler parked on the right side of the street and came to a halt. Up ahead of us, the sedan had stopped too, and three men in dark overcoats were piling out. The assassin squad.

I couldn't stay in the cab. Penned up in there, I'd be as difficult a target as fish in a barrel. The cabbie was still yelling frantically ten seconds after the crash, but I was already pushing down on the door handle and stepping out of the hack on the right-hand side, my gun in my hand. "Get down," I shouted to the cabbie. He leaped for the floorboards and I slammed the door. A moment later, there was the sound of crunching glass as a bullet spanged through the left-hand rear window of the cab, thunking into the upholstery.

I crouched down behind the cab, hoping that the bullets would keep away from the gas tank. I heard the cabbie mumbling prayers.

I wanted to mumble a few myself.

TWELVE

It's just like they say in those advertisements for the newspaper. You can't draw a crowd in Philadelphia no matter what you do. Especially on a Sunday night in the downtown district. We had the street to ourselves—me and the cabbie and the three hoods. I guess everybody within earshot must have figured that the banging noises were just auto exhaust.

Keeping an eye on three guys at once isn't easy, especially when they want to murder you. They kept trying to creep around behind the cab that I was using as a shield. Minton and two others, and all three of them armed. Another shot smashed through the body of the taxicab. I heard the cabbie cursing and moaning.

So far I hadn't fired a shot. I knew I had to make them all count. But I got my money's worth out of the first one I fired. One of Minton's hoods was trying to come at me from the side, where I was vulnerable for a couple of feet between the parked cars.

I got my head down just in time to miss a slug that whizzed past and plonged against a lamp post behind me. Then I shot him. I was shooting to disable, not to kill, but he made a clumsy attempt at ducking, and it cost him. I leaned up over the tailfin of the taxi and squeezed off a shot that should have gone through his right shoulder, but he was starting to slide away as I fired, and the shot went through the middle of his chest instead. He looked surprised and started to fold up, blood spilling out of his mouth.

I didn't stop to apologize for my lousy marksmanship. Before the corpse had hit the pavement, I was going for the other two.

They were playing it cagy. Minton was squatting behind a Volkswagen across the street, aiming over the snub nose of the little car and trying to take me apart with a lucky shot. The goon was about twenty feet further down the block, edging around the sedan and trying to slip onto my side of the street and pick me off from my left. As the two of them got further and further from each other, it got harder for me to watch them both. Which was what they wanted.

They were about thirty feet apart now, and at right angles to each other. Minton fired twice, missing both times but not by much. Then they wised up and began alternating their fire, Minton taking a shot and then the gorilla.

I held up on returning. I only had one gun, and the only place you can reload during this kind of gun battle is in the movies, where they're firing blanks anyway.

But the gorilla was getting bolder and bolder; I drove him back to cover with a quick shot past his left ear, then pivoted and creased the top of the Volkswagen, though unfortunately not the top of Minton. I wondered just how long I was going to hold out before a platoon of cops arrived and closed us all out.

Then the goon got too bold. He made a wide sweep to

my left, figuring to slip between the taxi and the car it had ploughed into, and pick me off easily while I was busy with Minton. Only Minton neglected to keep me busy at just that precise moment. He stopped firing. I turned to my left, and there was the gorilla, plain as day and looking pretty damned surprised. I squeezed off a shot, taking him in the upper pectoral muscle, and he yelped and hit the street.

Now there was just Minton.

And Minton used brains for the first time since I had known him. He stopped aiming for me and went for the gas tank of the cab. He got it on the second try, and I heard a swoosh and knew we were in for some flames.

Opening the cab door, I looked in at the driver huddling under his steering wheel and yelled, "They got the tank! We're on fire!"

"I'm staying here, mister."

"Don't be an idiot. They aren't shooting at you! You want to roast?"

He was too scared to budge. I couldn't stop to argue with him, so I grabbed him and hauled him out of the cab, thankful that Minton's bright idea hadn't occurred while the odds were still three to one. The rear of the cab was blazing now. I pushed the dazed cabbie out onto the sidewalk and looked up at Minton. He was waiting for me to get away from the flaming taxi. I had to risk it. I darted out into the open, streaking for cover, and fired one of my two remaining shots in his direction. It missed. I heard Minton laugh, and just as I slid down behind another car he edged out into the clear himself, and I wasted my last shot on him.

My gun was empty. And Minton knew it.

The taxi was an inferno now, and the other car was about to go up, and in a couple of minutes the block would be full of police and fire engines and whatnot. But it didn't look like I'd be concerned with that. Minton had me now. He came across the street, gun drawn and ready. I crouched down behind the car that now shielded me.

He said, "Here's where you get it, Lowney—or whatever your name is. You really put me down, didn't you? Only I'm going to get you, now. I'm going to make you walk right into that cab and roast to death. You hear me, man? Come on out from behind that car. Don't make me shoot you, man. Don't spoil my fun."

I started to figure the odds on a *banzai* charge that might catch Minton off-balance. They weren't very good. But then I discovered that I had an ally I wasn't even counting on: the cabbie.

Seeing his cab go up in flames must have unhinged him. I was getting ready to make my leap toward Minton when the hackie let out a wild bloodcurdling scream and charged forward.

Minton turned in astonishment, firing as he did, and the shot practically took the cab driver's midsection apart. But by that time I was on my way toward Minton. I hit him hard, grabbing for the gun at the same moment, and wrenched it from his hand. At this final humiliation Minton practically shrieked in rage; he came at me, hands turning to claws, and I lifted one from the sidewalk, connecting solidly with his jaw.

I hadn't intended what happened next. He went staggering back, tried to grab hold of empty air, and fell into the blaze of the taxicab. There was one muffled wail, and he disappeared in flames.

No matter how tough you are, no matter how much of a worm the man was, you don't like to see anyone die that way. Even if he had just tried his damnedest to send you out the same way. I didn't stand around delivering a eulogy, though. Someone in one of the adjoining buildings had long ago given a fire alarm, and I heard sirens. Police sirens, maybe, as well as the fire engines. I had to get moving.

The entrance to the Bingham was three-quarters of a block ahead of me. There was nothing between me and it except some closed stores and the entrance to the hotel parking lot. I flew down the block and stopped short in front of the entrance. It was one of those underground garages, with a staircase going down into it and rising up into the hotel itself. Midway up the landing, there was a washroom. I stepped in, found a booth, and locked it.

I was drenched with sweat, and breathing hard. I looked at my watch, for some reason, and made the startling discovery that the entire battle had lasted just about two and a half minutes. I wouldn't have thought it had been less than fifteen. But your time-sense has a way of playing tricks when people are shooting at you.

I waited in the booth for five minutes while my heartbeat got back to normal and my breathing became regular again. Then I washed up, combed my hair, adjusted my tie, holstered my gun in its snug hidden holster, and stepped out of the washroom. I walked up the spiral catwalk and into the Bingham hotel lobby.

But the lobby was just about deserted. Everybody—bellhops, desk clerk, guests—all were clustered on the steps of the side entrance, peering out. I walked over and joined them, shouldering my way toward the street until I got a view of what was going on down the block.

It was pretty damned hectic.

The narrow street was jammed with official vehicles. A fire engine was there, and a bunch of police cars, and an ambulance. Policemen and firemen were milling around everywhere. The fire was out, but smoke was coming up strongly.

I turned to my neighbor in the crowd and said, "What happened?"

"You mean you missed all the shooting?"

"Shooting?" I said, awed.

The man nodded. "There was some kind of gun battle down there. Two gangs trying to rub each other out, or something. And some parked autos were set on fire by the bullets."

"Imagine that," I said. "Not even a Sunday is sacred to those people. I hope they all were killed."

"Looks that way," my new friend observed contentedly. "They were really blasting away at each other. It was all over in a hurry, but they say there were bodies lying everywhere on the street."

I muttered some expression of alarm and worked my way back through the crowd and into the lobby. The excitement was over, now, and the crowd was breaking up. What I wanted more than anything else right now was a drink, but this was Philadelphia on a Sunday, remember?

I got into the elevator.

The elevator boy was still jubilant about the gunfight. "Boy, we haven't had this much fun since the Paratroopers had their reunion here in '55," he said. "And two guys got drunk and jumped down the stairwell. Without chutes. What's your floor, mister?"

"Eight," I said.

The elevator rose. He went on, "I missed all the shooting. Happened so fast nobody really saw it, they tell me. But those cars really blazed, like I mean *blazed*! And blood all over the street. Here's your floor, mister."

I walked down the quiet corridor to Chavez' corner suite. Up here, in the peaceful reaches of the Bingham, the world of bullets and blazing cars seemed very very far away. I hesitated for a moment, listening outside Chavez' door. I heard nothing. I knocked.

"Who's there?" Chavez called.

"Joe Manners."

"Hold on a sec, Manners," Chavez said. After a moment, he opened the door, looking at me uneasily. He was wearing a silk dressing gown, Japanese-looking, expensive-looking. "Come on in," he muttered.

"Thanks." I stepped inside and he locked the door. The first thing that met my eye was a tray with some lovely things on it: a fifth of tequila, a couple glasses, some lemon.

Chavez seemed surprised to see me. He dithered around, saying nothing in particular, and after a minute of this I said, "How about offering your partner a drink?"

For a second he seemed to have forgotten that we were supposed to be partners. Then his face brightened a little and he laughed. "Oh, yeah. Sorry, Manners. Help yourself, why don't you?"

I poured out a shot of tequila and cut myself a slice of lemon. I said, "You didn't have any of this stuff last night, man. And the package stores aren't open on Sundays in this town. Where's your magic wand?"

"He's running the Number Three elevator," Chavez said. "I wasn't going to wait for Monday for a drink. I gave him a ten and he got me the fifth." Chavez chuckled. "You know something funny? I paid him with one of the samples Klaus gave me!"

"Why the hell not?" I asked, grinning. "They're as pretty as real money, and a lot cheaper." I lifted the glass to my lips. Straight tequila is not one of my most favorite tipples, but under the circumstances I wasn't going to argue much. I put the shot away in one good gulp, exhaled, bit into the lemon.

"You look like you enjoyed that," Chavez said.

"I did."

"Have another."

"Not right away." I put down the glass. "I needed that. I needed it bad."

"You look kind of shaky," he said.

"I feel kind of shaky. Didn't you hear any of the fireworks?"

"What you mean?"

"I guess you're on the wrong side of the hotel. There was a little shooting going on downstairs."

"Who?"

"Minton and two goons. They followed my cab over here, sideswiped us, started blazing away. They killed my cabbie, and set the cab on fire. I shot the two goons and knocked Minton into the fire. I guess he must have burned to death."

Chavez stared at me, not knowing whether or not to believe me.

He said, "You talk about it like you had a flat tire on the way over here."

"What do you want me to do? Have hysterics?"

"You sure Minton's dead?"

"I wouldn't swear," I said. "But he isn't in good shape if he's alive. I know I killed one of the goons. I just winged the other one."

Chavez moistened his lips. "That Minton wanted to get you, eh, Joe?"

I shook my head. "Not Minton. Klaus was the one who wanted to get me. But I got a plan for fixing things for Mr. Klaus."

THIRTEEN

Chavez looked troubled. I couldn't blame him. He and Klaus had probably agreed on my removal early this afternoon, and instead of hearing about my death Chavez now found himself getting drawn into a plan to dispose of Klaus. He was in a tricky spot.

He said, "What kind of plan?"

I sat back, crossed my legs, and casually poured another tequila. It's dusty-tasting stuff and the texture is thick and oily, but if you drink it down fast enough the taste and the texture don't really matter. And the effect is just fine. I put the shot away.

Then I said, "Can you give me one good reason why you ought to pay a rake-off to Klaus for using his product, when you could be turning the stuff out yourself?"

"He's got good plates."

"Agreed," I said. "But you aren't thinking, Chavez. Klaus' outfit is a bunch of second-raters. They've been trying to kill me for a couple of days, now, and they haven't even come close. We can take them."

His brows furrowed until they met right over the bridge of his nose. "What you mean, take them?"

I hunched forward. "I've got friends in New York who want to finish off Klaus."

"Say more, man."

I gave him the big smile. "These boys from New York, they're minded to grab Klaus' plates and his engraver and set up business for themselves in New York. I have a feeling it'll be a lot easier to do business with them than with Klaus." I eyed Chavez carefully. "Suppose we help my New York friends take Klaus out," I said.

"In return for that favor, they give us a set of plates. Then we go out west and print the queer ourselves, and no rake-offs to anybody. You interested, or would you rather keep on doing business with Klaus?"

A slow smile appeared on his face. His eyes glittered greedily. "I'm interested."

"I figured you'd be."

"How are you going to work it?" he asked.

I said, "Simple. We arrange a little ambush. Klaus owns a roadhouse on U.S. 1, south of Philly. A little side operation of his. Tomorrow night you get Klaus to take you out there."

"Suppose he doesn't want to?" Chavez asked.

"You *make* him want to. Tell him you want him to show you a good time. He'll take you. You hang around late, till closing time. That's three in the morning. Meantime I get in touch with my New York fellows. Three or four of them come down to Philly and show up at the roadhouse at closing time. The place is almost deserted. You and Klaus step out on the front porch, and suddenly you step back inside. My guys open fire and cut Klaus down. Good?"

"Okay. What then?"

"Then we high-tail it back to town and grab Klaus' engraver and the plates, and we scram."

"Where do you get the engraver?"

"I know where," I said. "They've got him stashed in the suburbs. I've seen the place. It's guarded by Klaus' goons, but they won't be much of a problem. We break in, get what we want, and by breakfast time we're in New York with the plates and everything. We collect our reward for luring Klaus to the roadhouse—a set of plates—and we head for the Coast. And set up production. A fifty-fifty split, partner."

"Sixty-forty my way," Chavez said immediately. "Without me you'd never get anywhere."

I shrugged. "Okay, sixty-forty. You like the deal, though?"

"I like it just fine," he said "Klaus won't."

"That's tough on Klaus. We'll send flowers to his funeral."

Chavez laughed. It was a small-boy giggle, an *Aren't-we-devils?* kind of laugh. I gave him a close, searching look, wishing I could see behind that smooth face and find out what he was really thinking. This was the critical turning-point of the whole operation, right here and now. If I had misjudged Chavez, everything would collapse. Would he go through with the doublecross of Klaus? Or would he doublecross Joe Manners instead? The direction he decided to lean in was crucial.

He poured himself a liberal slug of tequila and belted it down like someone who'd been drinking the stuff from the cradle. Then he said quietly, "Let me get all this straight. Tomorrow night I ootz Klaus into taking me to this roadhouse of his. Your boys are waiting there at three in the morning. When Klaus steps outside, they gun him down."

"Check."

"Then we pick up the engraver and clear out."

I nodded. "That's all there is to it."

He said speculatively, "How big a mob is coming down from New York?"

I shrugged and said, "I told you. Maybe three or four guys. Half a dozen at the very most. As long as Klaus doesn't bring his whole goon squad along, there won't be any trouble."

Chavez smiled peculiarly. "Don't worry. There'll just be me and Klaus and maybe a chauffeur. I'll make sure of that. Where will you be?"

"In the car with the New York guys. I have to meet them in town and guide them out to the roadhouse."

"Who is this bunch, anyway?"

"Fellow name of Litwhiler," I said. "An old enemy of Klaus'. Litwhiler's in the jewelry trade, and turns out queer on the side. But his product can't compare with Klaus', because they don't have the engraver. So he's anxious to take Klaus over."

"Okay," Chavez said. "It's all set. We put the nix on Klaus and get the plates from this guy Litwhiler. That's a lot better than paying Klaus royalties."

"Damn right it is," I chimed in.

"You trust Litwhiler to keep his end of it?"

"He won't cross us," I promised. "He knows what's good for him."

"Let's hope so," Chavez said. He looked at his wrist-watch. "Listen, Manners, I'm going to have to be impolite now. I'm going to ask you to leave."

"For why?"

"It's eight o'clock, and I'm expecting a chick here by eight-thirty," he said with a leer. "I'd sort of like to be alone when she gets here."

"Sounds like a reasonable suggestion," I said. I elbowed up out of the chair and reached for my coat. "Have fun, Chavez."

"I intend to. See you tomorrow night around three, Manners."

"Yeah. Tomorrow at three."

"I'll call you at the Penn Plaza if there are any hitches," Chavez said. "But I don't expect any. Take it slow, man."

"You too," I said, and ambled out.

I left the hotel by the side entrance and walked up the block to the scene of the shooting. Everything was calm and peaceful looking now. They had towed away the damaged cars, and all that remained to hint at the fracas were some oil-slicks in the gutter and a couple of splotches of blood on the sidewalk. Otherwise, the deadly calm of Sunday night in Philly had settled over the scene.

I hailed a cab and rode back to the Penn Plaza without any further incidents. Either Klaus had run out of goons or he had temporarily abandoned the idea of gunning me, because no snipers tried their skill on me as I got out of the cab and went into the hotel.

I checked at the desk for messages, hoping that Elena

Szekely might have tried to get in touch with me during the evening.

But she hadn't. For once, there were no messages for Vic Lowney, no calls, no anything. Which was too bad. It looked very much like I was going to have to go through with the operation tomorrow night without telling Elena in advance about the schedule of events.

Up in my room, I undressed and sprawled out on my bed in a pair of Lowney's fancy pajamas. I was keyed-up and starting to sprout a neat little headache. I'd been shot at more times in the past two days than in the whole last two months, and my nervous system was starting to gripe about it. I told it to shut up. Nobody shoots at post-office clerks, but I still wouldn't trade my job for theirs any day.

By way of relaxing, I snapped on the television set at random. The screen brightened into the nine-thirty news program, and an announcer with an earnest crewcut face stared out of the box at me and said ringingly, *"The serenity of the Sabbath was rudely shattered today by two separate outbreaks of old-style gang violence."* The screen now showed a view of the north end of City Hall, with a trenchcoated reporter standing on the spot where Carol had fallen. The news commentator went on, *"At half past four this afternoon City Hall was the site of the first incident. A pretty 28-year-old ex-nightclub performer stepped out of a taxi. Moments later, an automobile pulled up and four shots were fired. One bullet struck the girl in the back, and she died instantly, while the murder car sped away. The dead woman was identified as Miss Carol*

Champlain, a one-time dancer and striptease artist with reported underworld connections. Police speculate that jealousy was the motive behind Miss Champlain's murder."

City Hall now faded from the screen, to be replaced by a still of the street where Minton and his crew had tried to finish me off. The shot had been taken after the removal of the bodies, but three charred automobiles were still on the spot—the cab and two parked cars that had gone up too.

The announcer said, *"Then, three hours later, a sensational gangland battle in this quiet side street off Broad brought death to four, including taxi driver Rudolph Kleinfeld, 51, of Port Richmond. Three gangland figures also died. Frank Gozzi, 39, was found dead at the scene, while Paul Maher, 32, was found wounded and succumbed to shock and loss of blood an hour ago at Our Lady of Mercy Hospital. Both Gozzi and Maher had criminal records. The body of a third man was discovered in the flaming wreckage of Kleinfeld's cab, but has not yet been identified.*

"Police speculate that Gozzi and Maher had attempted to kill the unidentified third man, but died themselves, while their victim perished when a stray bullet ignited the gas tank of the taxi. Cab driver Kleinfeld evidently was shot while attempting to interfere in the encounter. But one puzzle has already presented itself: Both Gozzi and Maher were shot with slugs from a .38-caliber pistol, while the only guns found on the scene were .45s. Mr. Kleinjeld had been shot with a bullet of the latter caliber.

This has led police to suspect that a fifth man took part in the duel but slipped away after shooting Gozzi and Maher. In any case, this was the most violent Sunday afternoon Philadelphia has had since the spring of 1955, when—"

He mentioned some other case, and then the news focus shifted, first to some new Soviet space satellite and then to the afternoon pro football scores. I watched the screen without really watching, just letting the flickering images go past my eyes.

I had scored a clean sweep of the rubout trio, it seemed. Too bad about the taxi driver—who in his own panicky way had saved my life at the expense of his own. I guessed that there would be clashing of teeth over at Klaus' headquarters tonight over the new failure to dispose of me—at the cost of three men.

Klaus probably wouldn't worry too much about the loss of Minton; he had proved himself an incompetent too many times in the past week. But still, it was galling to lose three men and gain absolutely nothing at all.

And Carol gone too. So I no longer had any insight on what was going on at Klaus'.

I switched off the television set, even though it was only ten o'clock. But I wasn't going to get any sleep Monday night, and so I figured it was best to sack out early and face the next day with a clear head and steady hands. I was going to need both.

All the wheels were turning, now. Litwhiler coming down from New York—Chavez alerted to the double-cross—Klaus busily trying to rub me out.

Tomorrow everything would mesh. Maybe.

I got into bed and waited for sleep. But sleep was a long time in coming. Nor was it a very pleasant night of sleep I had, either, when I finally dozed off. There were dreams. I saw Carol Champlain coming toward me in the dark. She was stark naked, but there was a raw dripping cavity between her breasts, and she was shaking her head sadly as though regretting my failure to rub out Klaus before he got *her.* And then I dreamed of Minton, and there was the smell of roasting flesh in my nostrils.

There ought to be a law against dreaming. I woke up half a dozen times during the night. By the time morning came, I was more tired than when I had sacked out.

FOURTEEN

Monday.

My seventh day in Philadelphia.

The big day.

It started off slowly. I didn't want to leave the hotel, for a couple of reasons. The major reason was that I wasn't keen on exposing myself unnecessarily to a possible eradication attempt by Klaus. The minor reason was that I was still hoping Elena Szekely would try to contact me, and I wanted to be available when and if she did.

I had a leisurely breakfast in the hotel coffee shop and leafed through the morning papers. There was a big spread on the gang stuff, of course. A front-page picture three columns wide showed the taxicab on fire, hoses playing on it frantically, and a body sprawled next to it. The murder of Carol Champlain got a lesser spread, with a photo of her on one of the inside pages. And, of course, there were statements from the police commissioner and the mayor about how drastic steps would be taken to cut short this unprecedented crime wave before any more law-abiding citizens were jeopardized, etc., etc.

After breakfast I phoned Washington, collect. I spoke briefly to my man there, telling him that things were approaching their climax.

"Good," he said. "We can't hold Lowney much longer

without all kinds of complications. He's been howling for a lawyer all week."

"Let him howl," I said. "What does he think this is, a democracy?"

"When do you think you'll be finished down there?"

"By dawn tomorrow," I told him. "One way or another— I'll be finished here."

I must have used up four hundred cigarettes that day, waiting for the minutes to tick past. By mid-afternoon my fingers were stained with nicotine and my throat felt like it had been left out in the Arizona sun for a few days. But there was nothing that I could do except smoke. And pace. And wait.

No word from Elena Szekely. I wrote her off. The caper tonight would have to be carried out despite not hearing from her.

I didn't hear from anybody. Not Chavez, not Klaus, not anyone. I was the forgotten man of Philadelphia. After the hectic pace of the first few days of this assignment, today was a drag.

At half past five the telephone rang. I was at the other end of the room, staring out the window at the garage across the street. I crossed the room in three big bounds and grabbed up the receiver, hoping it was Elena Szekely calling.

"Hello?"

The Penn Plaza switchboard operator said, "Mr. Lowney? I have a call for you from New York."

"All right," I said.

"Go ahead, New York," the operator chirruped.

There was a pause. Then Litwhiler's deep, commanding voice said, "Everything set for tonight, Lowney?"

"As set as can be."

"We're all ready too. We're going to leave New York at half past twelve tonight."

"How many of you?"

"Ten, including me. Two cars. You think that'll be enough?"

"Plenty," I said.

"Okay. Where do we meet you?"

"At the Penn Plaza," I said. "Just like we arranged the other day. Phone me from the lobby and I'll come right down."

"Okay. We'll be there around quarter to three," Litwhiler said. "Be seeing you then."

"Check, man. Quarter to three."

I put down the receiver, let it rest for a moment, and picked it up again. The hotel operator said, "Your number, please?"

"Connect me with the car-rental service in the lobby, will you?"

She did, and I said, "This is Mr. Lowney from room ten-sixty-six. I rented one of your cars Friday night, and I'd like to do the same tonight."

"Of course, sir. We can offer you your choice of Ford, Chevrolet, Oldsmobile—"

"Make it a Cadillac," I said. I needed a big, powerful car with plenty of reserve. "How late are you open?"

"Only until nine, sir."

"Have the car ready for me around nine, then. I'll want it overnight."

"Yes, sir. If you'll stop off at this desk about ten minutes to nine, I'll have the keys ready for you, and you can sign for the car then."

The next step on the agenda was to get packed. I trundled out the suitcases and got everything stashed away except the clothes I would need for the next twelve hours. When everything was packed, I phoned downstairs again—this time to the travel agency in the lobby. I had them book a flight to Washington, D.C. for me, on the first plane going out in the morning. They squirrelled around for a while, finally told me I had a seat on Flight 113, leaving Philly at 7:05 A.M. and arriving in the capital practically immediately afterward.

So far, so good. Continuing my exit arrangements, I had a bellhop sent up to carry my luggage to the hotel lobby. Pausing at the hotel desk, I said, "I'll be leaving you very early tomorrow morning, I'd like to check out and settle up now, and keep my room overnight."

"Of course, sir. What room is that?"

"Ten-sixty-six."

She found a big ledger, leafed through it, nodded. "Ah, yes. Mr. Lowney. I'll have to figure your charge as though it ran to noon tomorrow, Mr. Lowney."

"That's all right," I said. "It won't break me."

She figured out my bill—a full week, plus a small fortune in telephone calls and meals. It came to a couple of hundred dollars. I paid them in cash, *real* cash, and tacked another three figures onto the swindle sheet I'd be submitting, when and if.

"You just turn in your key whenever you decide to leave, Mr. Lowney," she told me. "There's somebody on duty all night."

"Right. I'm going to drop my bags off at the airline terminal now. It'll save time in the morning," I said, whistling for another bellhop.

The terminal was four blocks from the Penn Plaza. I took a cab over there, stood in line for a while, finally reached the check-in counter. I told the fellow on duty that I was ticketed for Flight 113 to D.C. the following morning, and I wanted to check my luggage in now,

He seemed a little puzzled at first, but I explained that I wouldn't find it convenient to bring the bags with me in the morning, and he okayed my request. He handed me my luggage tags and promised me faithfully that the bags would be transported to the airport and placed aboard my plane during the night.

It was time for dinner, now. I cabbed back to the Penn Plaza and treated myself to eight bucks' worth of rare, juicy filet mignon. I washed the meal down with an entire pot of coffee. My mind had to be clicking on all cylinders tonight, and I wasn't going to get very much sleep.

Everything was set for a quick departure. I racked my brains, trying to think of anything I had forgotten to take care of. But everything seemed under control. Everything, that is, except the human equation formed by Chavez and

Litwhiler and Klaus—the equation full of variables. I had done the best I could to shape that equation the way I wanted it. Whatever happened now was beyond my control.

At quarter to nine, I went down and picked up the keys to my car. I drove the Caddy around the corner into the hotel parking lot and left it there, telling the attendant I would probably want to pick it up around three in the morning.

Then I went back upstairs to wait.

It was a long evening.

I watched television and I smoked half a pack of cigarettes, and twice during the evening I phoned down to room service to have a pot of coffee sent up. The second time, though, I phoned for the coffee only to have something to do. I didn't *need* the coffee. I couldn't have been any wider awake, any more keyed-up, than I was by that time.

Midnight came and went. The idiot box was showing an old movie, a 1933 thing with Carole Lombard and John Barrymore, and I watched it absorbedly. At half past one, though, it was over. I turned the set off. I walked around the room, counting the number of paces the long way, then the short way.

This was the worst time, the waiting time. By now, I knew, Litwhiler was on the way. Two cars full of New York hoods were rolling southward along the Jersey Turnpike, past the sleeping towns, past the oil refineries and the farms. They were about halfway there now, I figured—just past New Brunswick, maybe.

Quarter to two. Two. Two-fifteen. Litwhiler was paying the toll, now. And they were leaving the Turnpike, heading through the side roads, through the back streets of Camden, across the Benjamin Franklin Bridge into Pennsylvania, down the broad expanse of silent avenues to the Penn Plaza—

Two-thirty.

Two-forty.

I checked my gun. It was oiled, loaded, ready for use. If I needed it. And I probably would.

Two-forty-five on the nose. The telephone rang, shattering the long silence.

"Hello?"

"Litwhiler here," the deep voice said.

"You believe in punctuality, eh, man? Right on the minute."

"I like to do things the right way, Lowney. We're waiting for you in the lobby."

"I'll be down in a minute," I said.

It took a while, at that hour, to get an elevator. But finally I did. I stepped out into the lobby and there was Litwhiler, looking suave and natty in his gray cashmere topcoat. There were two men with him, typical hoods with padded shoulders and shifty eyes. They looked like extras for some film about Al Capone.

"Where are the rest of them?" I said.

"Waiting outside with the cars." Litwhiler looked at his watch. "You figure forty minutes to get to the roadhouse from here, eh?"

"That's right."

"So we ought to show up there at just around half past three. You sure it'll be all closed up by then?"

"Positive. There'll be nobody there but the goons guarding the old man. It'll be a walkover, Litwhiler."

He nodded. "Let's get going, then."

I took the key out of my pocket. "Here," I said. "You'll need this to get in. The name of the place is the Casablanca, and—"

"Never mind that for now. Come on."

I looked at him in surprise. "Man, you got the wrong idea. *I'm* not going out there with you."

Litwhiler blinked in surprise. "The hell you're not, Lowney."

"I got other things to tend to," I said. "You take the key and bust in there yourself."

"Crap on that," Litwhiler snorted. "We aren't going to go roaming around the woods hunting for this place. You're going to show us exactly where it is. And then you're going to lead us inside and take us upstairs to where the engraver is kept. We don't even know what the old man looks like, Lowney. You're essential, get me? So come on."

There was cold menace in his hard little eyes. The two goons shifted their feet uneasily, as if a little bashful about having to commit mayhem in such a glossy new hotel lobby.

The lobby itself was practically deserted. There was a night clerk behind the desk reading the papers, a bellhop sitting near the front door, and a janitor swabbing the marble floor. But our conversation had been carried on in low tones, and nothing could be heard.

I said stiffly, "There wasn't anything in our arrangement that said I was going with you to the place, Litwhiler. I got other fish to fry tonight."

"*I* say you're going. If you want your dough, you will." He looked at his watch again. "It's eleven minutes to three. You're using up valuable time."

The two goons moved closer to me. One of them murmured in a thick, fuzzy whisper, "Look, bud, why doncha just do what the boss wants, huh?"

I was boxed in. The last thing I wanted was to go way the deuce out to the Casablanca tonight and get mixed up in whatever might be happening there. On the other hand, this might be one pretty good way of finding out who Chavez had decided to doublecross.

I scowled. "This is a pain in the neck, Litwhiler," I muttered irritably.

"You're a bigger one. Come on," he hissed. "Or am I going to have to make you?"

Giving him a dirty look, I said, "You win. Let's get the show on the road."

FIFTEEN

Two cars were parked right in front of the hotel—a huge Continental and a smaller, rather battered Buick. Both cars were full of hoods.

Litwhiler said, "We've got some room in the Continental for you, Lowney."

I shook my head. "I've got my own car in the parking lot here. I'd rather drive that."

Shrugging, he said, "Suit yourself. We'll follow along behind you. Phil, go with him."

Phil was a hulking ape, about six feet six, with long dangling arms. I went around to the parking lot, with the ape shambling along behind me. The night attendant brought the Caddy out front, and I got in back of the wheel. Friend Phil settled ponderously next to me.

"Jeez, mister, you got a pretty car," Phil rumbled as I got the Cadillac started.

"Glad you like it, pal."

"Musta cost a pretty penny, huh? Like ten grand, maybe?"

"Someone gave it to me for a present," I said. I swung the car around to the right, into the street. The Continental and the Buick both started their engines. I drove slowly west along Market Street, following the signs until I came to U.S. 1. The Continental was right behind me, with the Buick bringing up the rear.

Phil was a friendly sort of ape. He praised the car for a while. I guess I didn't make much attempt at keeping my end of the conversation going, because after a while he said, "You mind if I turn on the radio, mister?"

I allowed as I didn't mind. Phil punched the studs with massive fingers and the radio came to life. With the unerring instincts of the natural-born cretin, he tuned in an all-night rock-and-roll station on the first try.

The Cadillac had speakers in front and behind the rear seat, and so all the way down to the roadhouse we were entertained by kiddie-crap in hi-fi. Phil sat there ecstatically, humming tunelessly to himself and jigging around in his seat. I was glad he was happy.

I took it slow, watching both sides of the road as we drove south on Route One. After all, I had never so much as laid eyes on the place I was supposedly so familiar with. It wouldn't look good if I shot past it by accident and wound up in Delaware.

Luck was with me. I spotted a road sign in a bend in the road that said:

ONLY FOUR HUNDRED YARDS TO

THE

CASABLANCA

DINING ⁕ DRINKING ⁕ DANCING

I stopped the car. Behind me, the Continental and the Buick pulled up. Litwhiler hopped out of his car and came jogging up to me.

"Why are you stopping here?" he asked me.

I pointed to the sign. "I just wanted to let you guys know we were close."

"Four hundred yards, huh? Okay. I'll tell the boys to drive slow and quiet."

He returned to his car, and I got the Caddy going again. We glided forward at twenty-five miles an hour, and in a couple of minutes the Casablanca came into view. It was a big Colonial-style farmhouse, set back a little bit from the road, with a big parking lot and signs on both sides of the road. I slowed practically to a crawl. The place was completely dark. I was going to have a lot to explain to Litwhiler if it turned out that nobody was there. But I doubted that it would work out that way.

A couple of butterflies started flapping in my stomach as I eased the car into the Casablanca's parking lot. The wheels crunched on the gravel. There were no other cars in the lot, but that didn't mean a thing; there seemed to be more parking space in back, and if Klaus was here he probably would have his car back there.

The Continental pulled up alongside me. The Buick likewise. We killed the motors. Everything was very, very quiet.

Rolling down his window, Litwhiler stuck his head out and whispered to me, "Okay, Lowney. You've got the key. Let's all go open the door."

I nodded. I got out of the car, and Phil did the same. I shut the door carefully. The rest of Litwhiler's mob now left their cars. Everybody was looking at me, waiting for me to go open the door.

I took the key out of my pocket, hefting it a moment. "Come on," I whispered. "Follow me."

Eleven strong, we tiptoed toward the dark, shuttered roadhouse. It was perhaps thirty yards from the parking lot to the front door. Our feet kept crunching on the gravel, no matter how carefully we walked. My throat was dry. This was the moment, I thought, that would tell the tale. Maybe. If Chavez had failed to come across, my whole grand plan would dissolve into soggy anticlimax. And I'd have a rough time with Litwhiler when we smashed into an empty place.

There weren't any anticlimaxes.

There was a big blazing climax.

When we were still fifteen yards from the door of the house, the upstairs lights suddenly went on. And Klaus' men began blazing away at us with machine guns.

It was like hitting the beach at Anzio. One moment everything quiet, the next a hell of sizzling fire. I was the only one at all prepared for it. The second the lights went on, I turned and broke for the parking lot and safety.

Behind me, Litwhiler's men were screaming and dashing for cover. Somebody in the roadhouse saw me and tried to cut me off; a barrage of tommygun slugs stitched a line in the gravel a couple of feet behind me, but I got clear just in time.

Jumping into the Cadillac, I got the engine started and looked out at the scene in front of me. It was pretty frightful. Three of Litwhiler's men were lying in front of the road-house, just about cut to ribbons by the hail of gunfire. The rest had avoided being hit in the first barrage. Some of them had jumped to the side of the roadhouse; others, like me, were racing back to the parking lot.

But it wasn't all one-sided. As I turned the motor on, I saw one of Litwhiler's men fire into an upstairs window, and a Klaus goon came toppling out, tommygun and all, to land on the ground with a meaty thud. And I heard Litwhiler's booming basso: "Set fire to the place, guys! Burn the bastards out!"

I began to back the Caddie out of the lot. Suddenly one of Litwhiler's men popped up in front of me, waving a cannon wildly.

"Hey! The doublecrosser's trying to get away!" he yelled. A slug whizzed through the windshield, landing harmlessly in the upholstery. One hand on the wheel, I fired with the other. The shot caught the hood in the throat, and he went down fountaining blood.

I didn't stop to see what happened next. I wheeled the car around and headed north on Route One as fast as I knew how, while the carnage raged merrily behind me. I felt a blissful wave of pure relief. There was one less unknown in the equation. Chavez had come through as expected.

He had agreed to lead Klaus into ambush. But, of course, he was much more interested in disposing of me than of Klaus. So after I had left him, he had probably contacted Klaus and told him about Litwhiler's ambush scheme. And Klaus had been ready for Litwhiler.

With luck, Litwhiler's gang and Klaus' would eliminate each other in the catfight down at the Casablanca.

That was fine with me. It costs money to prosecute people, and it costs more money to maintain them in the jug. As a taxpayer myself, I'm always happy to see potential jailbirds save all that expense by eliminating each other beforehand.

And while all the foofaraw went on down at the Casablanca, I'd have a chance to finish off the operation by grabbing old Szekely. It was too bad I hadn't had some way of warning Elena of what I was up to. But I would have to manage anyway, now.

I kept my eyes peeled for a police call box as I sped through the quiet suburban streets. I found one, finally, and pulled up at the curb.

Opening the box, I waited for some acknowledgment, and then said, "Hello. Listen, there's a gang battle going on at a roadhouse called the Casablanca, on Route One down near Lansdowne. The Klaus counterfeiting gang is involved, and a rival gang from New York. You can make some very important arrests if you get moving."

I hung up without waiting for a reply, and got back into the car. Fifteen minutes later, I was in downtown Philadelphia, and then I was heading up into the residential area where Klaus kept the Szekelys cooped up.

It was a little after four in the morning when I reached the house. The street was as asleep as a street can be. There wasn't a light on anywhere in the block. I left the Caddie parked out in front of the house and walked up to the door.

I rang the bell.

Half a minute passed. Nothing happened.

Then the view-slot in the door opened, and a bloodshot eye peered out at me.

"Yeah?" came the suspicious grunt.

"Open up," I snapped. "I just came from Klaus. He sent me to tell you guys something."

A lid descended over the bloodshot eye in a perplexed frown. Evidently the goon decided it was safe to let me in, though, because after another moment I heard the sounds of a chain being lifted and a bolt being drawn back. The door opened.

I was face to face with one of Klaus' more unsavory goons. I stepped inside and the .38 was in my hand, pressed right up against the goon's chin, and I said softly, "You just play it cool or I'll splatter your brains all over the county, bud."

"Who—what—?"

"Never mind. Where are your buddies?"

"There's only one. He's—inside—"

Only he wasn't. He was standing in the doorway of the living room, looking mystified.

"Hey, Jack, I heard the doorbell ring," he began. "Hey, who's—?"

The next second he saw the gun and went for his own. I didn't let him finish the motion. I fired right past the first goon's ear, and the other one folded up on the carpet with lead in his belly.

Jack was shivering, now. "Listen, m—mister, I ain't gonna try anything—"

"That's smart, Jack. Where's the old man and his daughter?"

"Upstairs."

"Thanks," I said. "And what's that over there?"

I pointed, and he turned his head to look, and I clipped him across the back of the skull with the butt of my gun. It made a satisfying thunking sound, and he dropped like a bunch of old rags. I fished the gun out of his pocket, removed the cartridges, and left it and him lying on the carpet. He would be out for three or four hours, I figured, and that was more than enough.

His pal was dead. A quick look told me that, and I didn't waste any time with first aid. I waited a moment or two, just in case Klaus had any more hoods on guard duty, but none appeared. I sprinted upstairs. "Elena?" I yelled.

She didn't answer. I called out again. "Elena, it's me, Vic!" She couldn't possibly have slept through all the ruckus downstairs. I switched on the light in the upstairs hall and pushed open the door of the first room I came to. It was a bedroom—Elena's bedroom. Only no Elena. A pair of gauzy pajamas and a bathrobe lay on the rumpled bed.

Frowning, I went into the next room and turned on the light.

Old man Szekely was there.

He was sitting up in bed, a short pink-cheeked man with a fringe of white hair around his ears. He was positively shaking with terror, and I realized I was still holding my gun. I holstered it quickly.

"Don't worry," I said. "I'm here to free you, not to harm you."

He shook his head dismally and muttered something in Hungarian. I smiled and shrugged. He continued to mutter.

I signaled to him. "Come on. There isn't much time. Let's get out of here."

I pulled him out of the bed. He stood in the middle of the floor, sleepy, pathetic, a tired old man scared out of his senses. I opened a dresser drawer and threw a shirt and some underwear at him. "Get dressed," I shouted, pantomiming it roughly. He didn't budge. He just stood there and trembled.

I couldn't afford to wait any longer. Hoping he'd have enough sense to get his clothes on himself, I rushed out of the room and downstairs. The plates were in the basement, Elena had said. I had to get them. And I had to get them fast. I had no guarantee that all the rest of Klaus' manpower had been tied up in the gun battle at the Casablanca.

SIXTEEN

Neither of the hoods had gone anywhere. The dead one was still dead, quietly puddling blood into the carpet. The other one, Jack, was fast asleep. I stepped over him and went into the hallway that led to the kitchen. I found the staircase to the cellar, and went down.

It was dark down there. I struck a match and found the light switch. It wasn't smart to blunder around in the dark in a possibly booby-trapped basement.

The light went on slowly—fluorescents. I whistled in awe when I could finally see. Down here was Ye Olde Compleat Printshop. There was a goodly sized flatbed press, bales and bales of paper, and, in the back, a desk ringed with an elaborate set of engraving tools. A monstrous steel cabinet with a combination lock no doubt held the finished product.

I didn't have time to bother opening the cabinet. Instead, I gathered up the plates on the engraver's desk, the cliche set in the press, and one package of blank paper. That was enough to prove the case against Klaus. The local police would have to take over the job of confiscating the press. Assembling my little bundle, I trotted back upstairs and ran out to the Cad with it. I dropped the stuff on the back seat and returned to the house.

Upstairs, the old engraver was sitting on the edge of his

bed staring at the clothes I had thrown him. He was still in his pajamas. He seemed dazed and baffled by it all.

"Dammit, I told you to get dressed!" I said.

He looked up woefully and replied in Hungarian. At least I guess it was Hungarian. But there isn't a drop of Magyar blood in my veins, nor had Grandma ever told me I'd have any need for knowing Hungarian when I grew up. I couldn't speak a word of it, not even "What a fine morning this is" or "This is the pen of my aunt." And Szekely probably knew only a smattering of English, and such smattering as it was had all vanished under the shock of my arrival.

So we had a communication problem.

I tried pantomime again, but he couldn't—or wouldn't—get the drift of what I was trying to tell him. After a few minutes of energetic charades, I decided I'd simply have to dress him myself. It was cold and windy outside, no night for taking a man of sixty outdoors dressed in pajamas. And I couldn't waste much more time coaxing him to get dressed.

So I dressed him.

There are techniques you learn for making unwilling people hold still, and I used them. Even so, he gave me plenty of trouble. Not that he fought me—he wasn't a very strong man—but that he didn't cooperate. Try to get clothes on and off a limp scarecrow some time and you'll see what I mean. It's even harder when the scarecrow keeps wriggling and making vague gestures of alarm and despair and fright.

But finally I had him dressed and his feet stuffed into shoes. I bundled him into a heavy coat, hooked my arm through his, and we started downstairs. We were midway down the landing when I heard a car door slam just outside the house.

I took my gun out and pocketed it, keeping my hand in the pocket too. We went on down the stairs. Just as we reached the next-to-last step, the front door of the house opened.

Elena Szekely walked in.

And Ricky Chavez walked in right behind her.

For one, long frozen minute we stared at each other across a gulf of perhaps twenty-five feet. At least, it seemed like a minute. It was probably only five or ten seconds at the most.

Then Chavez went for his gun. I didn't go for mine. I kept it in my pocket, with my hand on it, but I moved the old man over ever so slightly to make him a shield for the left side of my body.

"Put the gun away, Ricky," I said.

"You let go of Szekely first."

"Fat chance, man." I nodded toward the door. "I'm going to go out of here, and the old man is going with me. And you aren't going to interfere."

"Stop him," Elena said imploringly—and she was talking to Chavez. "Oh, stop him! He is kidnapping my father!"

"I'm rescuing him, Elena," I said.

She turned blazing eyes on me. "No, you are not! I know the truth about you now! This man has told me!

You are *not* who you said you are. You are completely unscrupulous and you wish to use my father yourself!"

The naked hatred in her face was an unpleasant sight. She was positively radiating contempt and rage at me. It was like looking right into an ultraviolet lamp.

I saw what had happened. Elena had despaired of ever getting any help from me, so, when Chavez appeared on the scene, she had gone to him with the same offer she had made to me. I wondered if she had been the "chick" Chavez had been expecting on Sunday night.

Probably she was. And if she had offered Chavez the same pay-in-advance scheme that she had offered me, why, that meant—

I scowled. Suddenly I hated Chavez as hard as I could hate a man.

He had taken advantage of her, nine chances out of ten. And then he had set up the ambush deal at the Casablanca, figuring that while Klaus and Litwhiler massacred each other out there he would quietly slip out here, guided by Elena, and abscond with the engraver, the plates, and— maybe—Elena herself.

A smart cookie, that Chavez. Why settle for a simple old doublecross if you can work a triplecross as well? The way he saw it, it was a good chance of dumping both Klaus and me—with Hammell's gang already frozen out of the scene—and setting up in business for himself using the talents of old Szekely.

Chavez said, "I'm warning you, Manners. Let go of the old man."

I squinted down the barrel of Chavez' gun and said, "You wouldn't risk shooting at me with him right here, would you?"

"I'm a crack shot, Manners. I'd risk it. And I'd nail you."

"You're bragging, man. You're just showing off for your girlfriend. But she won't like it if you kill her father by mistake."

His tan face showed pale, now. He hovered indecisively, and while he hovered I casually drew my hand out of my pocket.

I showed him the gun.

"You see this?" I asked him. "I've got one, too. And I'll use it. Get away from the door or I'll shoot the old man. He won't be any good to you *or* me if he's dead, Chavez. But if I can't have him, nobody will."

Elena's eyes were incredible, now. Cat-slits of fury and contempt. There was no little-girl innocence about her, now. I knew she would gladly have ripped my eyeballs out if I came within reach.

I nudged the old man. "Let's go," I said.

We took a step forward. Chavez' lips worked silently. I kept the gun angled up so it aimed right into old Szekely's right ear. Even if Chavez fired, I would automatically discharge a shot no matter where I was hit—and Chavez knew it. He was stymied. If he killed me, I'd kill the old man—and he'd end up with nothing but useless corpses.

Another step.

Another.

I was almost in the middle of the floor, now. Chavez

and Elena still hadn't moved away from the door. I gestured with a quick toss of my head.

"Get over there," I said. "Over by the bookcase, both of you. You're in my way."

Chavez didn't move.

I said, "Don't make trouble, man. You know you're stuck. Let's not have any needless fireworks around here. Just get yourself where I tell you to stand, and the old man will stay healthy."

"Manners, when I catch up with you I'm going to give you the works. We'll take you out into the desert and work you over inch by inch, and then—"

"Skip the details," I said. "You're wasting my time. Get over there."

"And if I don't?"

"Don't be a wise guy, Chavez."

He smirked obnoxiously. Leaning against the door frame, he said, "And suppose I just stand right here, smart boy? What are you going to do then?"

I scowled at him. "I'm going to count to ten," I said quietly. "If you're not out of my way and standing by the bookcase by the time I count ten, I'm going to kill the old man. You hear me, Chavez? I'll kill him. And the next bullet will be for you."

"You talk big, man."

"One," I said. *"Two. Three."*

Chavez looked uneasy. But he didn't move. He just stood there in the doorway, right in front of me, a gun in his hand, a cold smile on his face.

"*Four. Five.*"

He wasn't budging. I felt a chilly trickle of sweat running down my side. *Don't call my bluff, Chavez,* I prayed desperately. *Don't test me, you filthy scum. Please don't. Because then maybe one of us will have to die—or maybe more than one.*

I cleared my throat.

"*Six. Seven.*"

The corner of Chavez' mouth began to twitch. Next to him, Elena's face grew very pale. I kept the gun aimed right at the old man's head. He didn't seem to have any idea of what was going on, though the sight of all these guns had left him shaking like a poplar leaf out in the wind.

"*Eight.*"

And Elena snapped out of her trance. She plucked at Chavez' sleeve and whispered urgently, "Please. Please do as he says. He is insane. He will kill my father. Oh, please do as he says!"

"*Nine.*"

Chavez was weakening. His face was glossy with sweat, now. I was just drawing my tongue to the roof of my mouth to say *ten*, when he shook his head and grunted, "All right, Manners. You win this round."

He stepped quickly aside, going with Elena to the bookcase to the left of the door. Elena glared at me and said something low and virulent-sounding in Hungarian. I couldn't understand a syllable of it, but I was willing to bet it wasn't the sort of language a young lady of Budapest was supposed to know.

Swinging around to face them, and shifting the gun so I was covering Chavez instead of the old man, I backed out the door, practically dragging Szekely every inch of the way. I kicked the door shut. Then—still in reverse gear, holding the engraver in front of me in case Chavez got the bright idea of taking a potshot at me from the window—I backed down the front walkway and edged toward my car.

Getting Szekely inside was a complicated maneuver. I had to grope for the handle without taking my eyes off the house. I got the door open and nudged him inside. He collapsed limply on the seat. Then, scooting around the car, I slipped behind the wheel and got the car going. It picked up beautifully with a great throbbing hum of power. Szekely moaned limply and squirrelled down on the seat. Just as well, I thought. This way he'd be out of the line of fire in case Chavez pursued me.

The car pulled away.

Everything was set, now. Klaus and Litwhiler busy with each other at the roadhouse; plates and engraver safe in my car; Chavez left behind. The jaws of the trap had closed neatly.

Except for Elena.

She had messed things up slightly. I had failed to warn her of what I was up to—and she had rung Chavez in on me. Well, no helping that now. I tromped down on the accelerator. I had to get the old man to a police station and slip away without being noticed myself. In the morning, the Treasury men could claim the plates, confiscate the remaining supply of queer, and generally mop up the situation, with me well off the scene.

I had gone a little more than a block when I saw the car pursuing me. Chavez' car.

It was a rented Cadillac, just like mine except for the color. I could make out two forms in the front seat of the car. So he had brought Elena with him, the idiot.

A red light winked on in front of me. I hit the gas and shot right through it. Chavez did the same when he came to it. I had the speed up to fifty, now, which was about all I dared to go on narrow suburban streets, even at half past four in the morning. But Chavez was doing sixty. He was nibbling down the gap between us. And it's a lot easier to shoot ahead than behind when you're in a moving car.

I heard a pinging sound—a bullet striking the rear of the car square between the tailfins and plowing through the trunk to come to a halt harmlessly against the back seat. I glanced into the rear-view mirror and saw Chavez leaning out his window, about to take another crack at me.

I nudged the wheel. The car cut sharply to the right. And a good thing, too, because I heard the zing of a bullet going through the air just to the left of the car.

Only a madman or a Californian would get into a running gun battle with helpless passengers in the cars. Chavez was a Californian, if not a madman. I pushed down on the accelerator, rammed the car up to seventy, and hoped for the best.

SEVENTEEN

It was a one-sided battle. I couldn't just lean over the side and take a potshot at Chavez with the car racing full tilt down a city street. All I could do was drive straight on.

I did. I had the not unreasonable hope that our antics would draw the attention of the police, who would head us off in motorcycles. Once we were all safely in custody, I'd be able to explain things, have Chavez put away, the Szekelys freed—

Only the Philadelphia police force, bless them all, was otherwise occupied this time. I roared down one street and up the next, Chavez hugging right along half a block behind me and popping off a shot every time he had a clear view, and nary a cop appeared.

I was sweating furiously. A bullet whined through the back window, continued on a wobbly course through the car, and passed to my right and out through the windshield.

There were two holes in the windshield now, the other one having been made by Litwhiler's thug an hour or so earlier, and a cold, fine stream of air whistled in. I was keeping count of Chavez' shots. That was the fifth one. Maybe he had a second gun, though. Or maybe he could get Elena to reload for him. With her background as a revolutionist, she probably would be able to cope with the job.

I kept turning street corners on a dime, thanking the auto industry for power steering and hoping that maybe at the high speeds we were going Chavez might shoot past without making the turn. No such luck. He drove like a devil, clinging right on my tail. Old Szekely was half-conscious, making small moaning sounds of terror.

The neighborhood was changing, now. We were out of the middle-income suburb where the Szekelys had been kept prisoner, and had now entered a much older section of town, where old brownstone houses were clumped together, only one design per block. Each block has a different style house, but there's that horrible uniformity all the way down the row, making you wonder if each house has the same people living in it.

I sped down one block, up another, trying to lose Chavez, just stalling for time until the police came after us and put an end to the wild chase.

And finally I did it. The neighborhood was a maze of identical streets, and I shot down one, made a right turn at the corner, took a left at the next block, and swung up on a diagonal back the way I came, only to see the reflection of Chavez' car zooming past the intersection without taking the turn.

Chavez was going to be sore at himself. By the time he got disentangled from the maze, I would be far across town—I hoped. What I wanted now was a police station. I cruised down a likely looking avenue in a hurry, but without finding either police or a station. The old man was in a bad way, whimpering like a frightened baby. I told him consolingly that everything was going to be all right, but he didn't seem to understand.

Only in Philadelphia is it possible to drive around for twenty minutes without seeing a living soul. The dash-board clock said five in the morning now. And I had yet to see anyone—not another car, not a policeman, not even a pedestrian.

I kept going down the avenue, looking at both sides of the street as well as watching the rear-view mirror in case Chavez was able to get back on the trail. And finally I found the precinct house I was looking for. I heaved a long sigh of relief.

"End of the trail," I said to the old man. "I'm going to turn you over to the police, now. They'll take care of you. Nobody will ever threaten you again."

He kept up the moaning. I pulled the car up in front of the police station and started to get out. And Chavez appeared.

It had been just luck that I had lost him, a dozen inter-sections back. Now luck had dealt *him* the extra aces. He came shooting out of a side street, saw me, and came to a squeaking halt. I ducked down behind the fender of the car, thinking, *Here we go again.* I was getting tired of duels in the street.

Chavez opened fire. He blasted away twice—telling me that he had reloaded or had an extra gun—and I heard Elena cry out to him, "Do not hit my father!"

Even in Philadelphia, you can't have a gun battle in front of a police station without getting *some* results. I took a quick glance behind me and saw lights going on in the precinct house. In another moment the street would be full of cops.

I saw Chavez, out of his car now, snaking around the rear for a clear shot at me.

I gave it to him. Free of charge.

I stood up and let him have his shot, and in the same instant I fired.

This round was mine.

His shot crashed into the trunk of the car. Mine took his head apart. When they train you, they tell you to aim for the body, never for the head—it's a bigger target. But all I had had to go for was his face. I hit it square on, and the slug ripped right on through and took the back of his head off, and he dropped without a sound. The next second, Elena's voice went up, a high, banshee-style wail of astonishing volume.

I didn't wait around to shake hands with the police and accept their congratulations for a job well done. As the gentlemen of the law made their belated arrival on the scene, I softly and silently vanished away, leaving them to confront one corpse, one hysterical girl, one semi-conscious old man, and two rented cars, one of which was full of interesting tidbits like perfect plates for ten-dollar bills.

I fled down the silent street, rounded the corner, ducked into an alleyway that went three-quarters of the way through the block, and cut sharply down the foul-smelling exit into a different street. This one was a good-sized avenue, the main drag of this particular section of town. It was just as dead as the side streets, except for a light on the next corner. Hallelujah. An all-night coffee shop.

My pulse was going triple time as I lunged across the street and into the doughnut dispensary. A truck driver was slouched over an omelet; the short-order cook, who was a young Puerto Rican with a hairline mustache, looked at me uncertainly—at five in the morning you never know who's going to come barging into your place—and said, "Yes, please?"

"A cup of coffee and a lettuce-and-tomato sandwich," I said. "I'll be needing your phone for a minute, too."

He waved me to the booth. I closed the door, dropped a dime in, dialed a cab service. The phone rang a dozen times before someone picked up. I said I wanted a cab, and gave my address.

"It'll be fifteen minutes to half an hour," I was told.

"I'll be waiting," I said, and hung up.

I dropped another dime in the slot and dialed for the operator.

"I want to call Washington, D.C.," I said. "Collect." I gave her the number. I waited a few minutes. Then I heard the operator say, "Long distance calling. We have a collect call from Mr. Victor Lowney, in Philadelphia. Will you accept the charges?"

"Yes," the deep voice answered. "Hello, Lowney."

I didn't apologize for waking him up. It's part of his job to be on call twenty-four hours a day at minimum. I said, "Everything's wrapped up here."

"Good deal." He didn't sound enthusiastic. In my line,

they don't pat you on the back just for doing your job the way they expect you to.

"Couple of details have to be touched up," I said. "You'll have to handle them."

"Go ahead."

"Klaus was involved in a gun battle just outside town about two hours ago," I said. "I left before it was over. He may be dead or perhaps he's in custody. You'll have to check with the locals in the morning."

"Right. What else?"

"The engraver. He's an old Hungarian named Szekely. I got him away from Klaus and dumped him in front of a precinct house, along with plates and other evidence." I gave him the address of the precinct house. "I also killed Ricky Chavez in the process of delivering the engraver to the cops."

"Chavez? How'd he get into this?"

"Tell you about it tomorrow," I said. "I'll be in Washington for breakfast. Meantime you phone up that precinct and tell them what they've got. You better tell them not to bother looking for Chavez' killer, either."

"I got you."

"Be seeing you," I said, and hung up.

My sandwich and coffee waited for me on the counter. The truck driver was gone; the short-order man hunched down sleepily and began to read a comic book.

I wolfed down the sandwich. "Slow night, huh?" I asked.

He looked up. "They are always slow. These are long hours, before dawn. Nothing ever happens."

I grinned. "Nope. Nothing ever happens."

Finishing the sandwich, I gulped down the coffee and left a bill on the counter. I walked out. The counterman was busy with his comic book.

I waited five minutes on the corner, amid absolute silence. Then a taxi pulled up, and the cabbie stuck his head out.

"You the fellow who phoned for a cab?"

"Yep."

"Where to?"

"Airport," I said.

We made the trip in silence. I leaned back in the cab, letting the tension drain out of me. It had been a long night. I was bone-tired. When I got to Washington, I figured I'd file my report and disappear somewhere for a week's sleep before taking my next assignment.

By quarter of six, we were at the airport. Out here, there were some signs of life. I checked in, making sure my baggage had reached its destination. Then I cooled my heels in the waiting room for what seemed like three years. At half past six—by that time the airport was almost crowded—came the announcement: "Flight 113 for Washington D.C., now boarding at Gate Seventeen. Flight 113 for Washington D.C.—"

I walked out onto the field. Dawn was just breaking over Philadelphia. The sky was gray, with faint streaks of pink near the horizon.

I wasn't sorry to leave the City of Brotherly Love. Not one little bit.

The plane was airborne precisely at 7:05, and a full house, too—businessmen mostly, with early appointments in the capital. It isn't much more than a hundred miles by air from Philadelphia to Washington, and by the time the stewardess had finished serving everyone their complimentary coffee and rolls, we were fastening our seatbelts and dipping down for the landing.

There were plenty of cabs waiting at the airport. I sat back and relaxed, watching the sun glint off the distant column of the Washington Monument as we crossed the Potomac. Up Constitution Avenue, then across to Virginia Avenue, and—stop. I won't go into details. But at five minutes after nine I was ushered into the familiar office. I was rumpled and sweaty and bloodshot, but the job was done.

"Hello, Nick," the boss said.

I grinned at him. "Say it again, will you? It's music to my ears—my real name."

"You don't hear it often, do you?" he chuckled.

"That's for sure," I said.

I lowered myself into the big plush armchair facing the desk, and helped myself to his cigarettes while he took a phone call. I marveled at the way he could look so fresh and crisp after having been dragged out of bed in the middle of the night.

He hung up the phone and gave me the million-dollar grin, and began to fill me in on the details that had developed while I was leaving Philadelphia.

Litwhiler and six of his goons had been killed in the

gunfight at the Casablanca, it developed. Five of Klaus' men had been killed too. Klaus himself had not taken part in the battle, but he had been there to gloat, and the police had nailed him. He was behind bars right now, along with the survivors of his gang and Litwhiler's, all awaiting arraignment on counterfeiting charges.

And Elena Szekely and her father were in custody, too, along with the evidence I had secured. The printing plant had been raided, and everything confiscated. Old Szekely would be needed to testify as a material witness against Klaus, but after the trial he would be a free man at last, and the government would make sure that nobody like Klaus ever showed up to threaten him again.

As for the real Vic Lowney, he was on his way back to California—but not as a free man. The Internal Revenue people had done some checking on him in his absence, and they had some matters they wanted to discuss with him.

So everything was wrapped up snug as a bug in a rug. Klaus canned, Litwhiler and Chavez and Minton defunct, the Szekelys free. My week in Philadelphia had been a bloody one, but fruitful.

And now?

A nice long rest-and-recuperation period. At least, that's what I thought until I brought the matter up.

The man on the other side of the desk gave me a warm, sympathetic smile. I knew that meant trouble.

He said, "Nick, I know exactly how you feel. And nobody could deny you've earned a vacation. But it happens that we're a little shorthanded right now, and I was just wondering if you wouldn't mind postponing your vacation by, oh, ten days, to tidy up a little job for us in the middle west? I won't insist, of course, but—"

What could I say?

So here I am. I've had two days to catch my breath and start fitting into my new role. The plane leaves at noon, with me aboard. And when the job is done, I get my vacation. If I'm still around to take it.

Oh, it isn't an easy life. But I don't mind. The job gets wrapped up and they hand you a new one, and you wonder what the *next* one's going to be like, and whether maybe it'll be the last. And you keep thinking, maybe this is the time to call it quits, get a transfer into some safer division, let somebody else do the dirty work now.

But deep down you know you won't ask for that transfer. You're going to keep walking the tightrope as long as you can. It's a cold job, a lonely job, and there are times when you hate it like poison. But it's the job they gave you. It's *your* job. And you know you're going to stick with it until they carry you out on a slab.

Afterword

The year was 1959. Dwight Eisenhower was in the final years of his presidency, the United States was making its early wobbly attempts to match Soviet achievements in launching space satellites, and the science fiction business had just tanked. I was 23 years old, three years out of college, and had been earning my living since graduation by traversing time and space for the readers of *Astounding Science Fiction*, *Galaxy*, *Infinity*, and a host of other magazines of that ilk—most of which had just gone out of business as a result of the distribution troubles that were plaguing many of the smaller magazine publishers that year. With science fiction seemingly on the verge of extinction, I needed some new markets for my work, fast, and very quickly I found them.

For the burgeoning flock of men's magazines I wrote allegedly non-fiction articles with titles like "The Secret Sex Rites of Uganda" and "Island of Love-Starved Women." For paperback houses like Midwood Books and Nightstand Books I wrote mildly erotic novels about suburban adulterers. And for a couple of crime fiction magazines called *Trapped* and *Guilty*, whose editor was also the editor of *Super-Science Fiction*, one of my regular science fiction outlets, I turned out a host of nasty little thrillers about hit men, juvenile delinquents, serial killers, and other unsavory sorts very different from the space explorers and time travelers I was accustomed to writing about.

Then I got a call from the editor of the s-f magazine *Fantastic Universe*, to which I had sold a number of stories in the past three years. His publisher was starting a companion magazine, he said, a crime fiction magazine, which, in the old-line pulp tradition, was going to feature in each issue the exploits of an undercover agent named Nick who traveled around the country masquerading as a criminal in order to snare evildoers. Did I want to write the first "Nick" story for the initial issue? I certainly did! So in September, 1959, I did a 6,000-word story called "Bridegrooms Scare Easy" for the new magazine. They liked it. They liked it very much, in fact, and immediately asked me to do a novel-length "Nick" story for them. I wrote it the very next month.

Unfortunately, the ongoing distribution crisis did in both *Fantastic Universe* and its new companion magazine a couple of months later. I did get paid for my novel, but it never was published. I put the manuscript away, forgot about it, and went back to my suburban adulterers and my virile tales of exotic adventure ("Opium Den in Vietnam," etc., etc.). *Super-Science*, which had been one of my science fiction standbys, paying quickly and generously, was another victim of the 1959 publishing collapse. But its two companions, *Trapped* and *Guilty*, were still staggering on, and each month I would bring to the midtown Manhattan office of their editor, W. W. Scott, one or two crime stories, which he bought for a cent and a half a word—nice money at the time—and published under such bylines as "Dan Malcolm," "Ray McKensie," and "Ed Chase." He never rejected a one.

A word about W. W. Scott seems appropriate here. He was a veteran pulp editor who looked to be seventy or eighty years old, though probably he was 55 or thereabouts. His voice was a high-pitched cackle; he had a full set of top and bottom dentures, which he didn't always bother to wear; and I never saw him without his green eyeshade, which evidently he regarded as an essential part of the editorial costume. I was a good deal less than half his age, but we became friends, of a sort. He was always glad to see me and told me many a lively tale of earlier days in publishing.

One day in 1962—*Trapped* and *Guilty* were tottering on the brink of extinction, now—Scottie told me that he wanted to try a desperate last-gasp experiment. Instead of running ten or twelve short stories in an issue, he would use one long novel, with a couple of shorts as fillers, and redesign the cover to make it look like a paperback book rather than a magazine. Could I write a 45,000-word crime novel for him, more or less overnight? Well, yes, I could, because I suddenly remembered my unpublished undercover-agent novel of a couple of years earlier, sitting there in my file cabinet. I dug it out, brought it to him the following week, collected another $800—with a purchasing power of at least ten times as much in modern money—and it was published in the November, 1962 *Trapped* under Scottie's gaudy title of "Too Much Blood on the Mink" and the "Ray McKensie" byline. That was, so far as I am able to discover, the last issue of *Trapped*, though I would not blame its demise on my novel. And I proceeded to forget the novel's existence for the next 49 years, until the resourceful Charles Ardai of Hard Case Crime found a copy of that old *Trapped* somewhere and suggested a reissue.

I got out my file copy of it, read it with great pleasure—after half a century I didn't remember a single thing about the story, so I came to it as though I were a new reader—and here it is once more, in book form for the first time, with a slightly altered title. By way of filling the book out I've included two short stories typical of the ones I was doing for *Trapped* and *Guilty* back then, each of them bearing some slight thematic resemblance to the novel. "Dangerous Doll," a Ray McKensie opus from the March, 1960 *Guilty*, runs a different riff on the counterfeiter plot, and "One Night of Violence," published as by Dan Malcolm in the March, 1959 *Guilty*, is a precursor of the gang-shootout scenes in *Blood on the Mink*.

Long, long ago. But when I read them again last month, half a century after the fact, I offered my younger self of that distant era a round of applause. He was still wet behind the ears, then, or so it seems to me from the vantage point of the senior citizen that he has become, but even back then, I think, he told a pretty good story. I hope modern readers will agree.

—Robert Silverberg
March, 2011

DANGEROUS DOLL

Eddie drove into Los Angeles around ten in the morning on a Tuesday. It was four days since he had left Chicago. He hadn't rushed the trip any—no more than eight or nine hours' driving a day. It was important to make a safe trip. There would be all kinds of hell to pay if he got into a crackup and the police found plates for ten-dollar bills in his car.

They were good plates. Real good. Almost as good as the real thing, the Chicago people had told Eddie. Eddie was just the courier. He carried the plates around the country for the Syndicate. The engraver, Klein, worked in Chicago. Eddie had only met him once. He was a tiny hunchbacked man with thick glasses and spidery fingers, and he was a wizard with an engraver's tools.

During the war, they said, Klein had been one of Hitler's engravers, preparing plates for counterfeit Allied money to mix up the war effort. After the war, Klein just took his skills and his tools to America.

Klein engraved the plates. Eddie delivered them. There was a press in Los Angeles, and one in Seattle, and one in Chicago, and one in Atlanta, and one in New York. The Syndicate covered the whole country. They turned out ones and fives and tens.

The ones were the easiest to pass, but you had to pass a

hell of a lot of them before it was worth the risk. Tens were harder, but the return was better. It cost about a nickel to print a fake ten-spot, all expenses included, and that left $9.95 profit every time you passed one.

Eddie didn't worry about the economics of it. The Syndicate paid him to carry the plates around, and they paid him in good honest twenty-dollar bills, guaranteed genuine.

It was warm in Los Angeles. Eddie liked that. It was winter back in Chicago, with snow piled deep on the ground and bitter winds forever sweeping in from the Lake, but here in L.A. the temperature was close to 70 and the tall spindly palm trees gave no hint of having endured a season of winter. It was too bad, he thought, that he couldn't stay longer than a few days. But the Syndicate wanted him to return to Chi as soon as he had made the delivery here. Klein would have another set of plates finished and Eddie would have to take them up to New York.

It was winter in New York too. Eddie looked forward to the day when he could quit the Syndicate and settle down in California, where winter never came.

He parked the car in front of a rooming house on Fifth Street just off Broadway. Making sure that the trunk was locked and all the windows were closed, he went inside and asked about a room.

"Sure we got rooms," the landlady said. "Three bucks a night, pay in advance. How long you figuring on staying, huh?"

Eddie shrugged. "Three or four days, maybe. Look,

here's ten bucks. That's for tonight, tomorrow, and the night after."

She wrote it down and gave him a dollar change. Eddie mentally added the dollar to his take for the trip. The Syndicate gave him two hundred bucks in queer tens as his expenses, aside from the actual delivery fee. Anything he could save out of passing the tens was pure profit for him.

Eddie went upstairs, looked over his room, nodded, and brought his suitcase up. The plates were in the suitcase. He unpacked, putting the little locked box containing the plates under a pile of shirts in his dresser drawer. He carefully arranged a thread that would tell him if anyone had been snooping in the room while he was away. Sometimes the landladies of these places liked to come in and nose around.

When everything was set, Eddie locked up carefully, went downstairs, and walked up the block to the nearest post office. He bought a 4¢ stamped envelope, took a sheet of paper from his pocket, and slowly printed in big block lettering the address of his rooming house and the number of his room.

He folded the sheet up, put it inside the envelope. He sealed the envelope and addressed it to a post office box number in Beverly Hills. He studied the sealed envelope for a moment, nodded, carried it over to the mail slot, and dumped it in.

He was sweating. This business of writing letters and mailing them always knocked him out. Eddie didn't go much for writing letters.

But now his part in the job was just about complete. Tomorrow the local Syndicate man would get the letter and would know instantly what it meant. Tomorrow or the next day or the day after, the Syndicate would send somebody over to the rooming house to pick up the plates. The messenger might be almost anybody, from the top West Coast man right down to the goons on bottom. Eddie didn't care who they sent.

The messenger would be carrying one half of a ripped-in-two ten-dollar bill, and if it matched with the half bill that Eddie was carrying in his wallet Eddie would turn over the plates, no questions asked.

And then Eddie would turn around and go back to Chicago, where he would collect thirty twenty-dollar bills for his courier services, and a new assignment to deliver plates.

He walked out of the post office and looked around. He was dressed in winter clothes, and he was sweating. He had nothing to do now, nothing to do but wait until the Syndicate got his address. They wouldn't receive it before tomorrow morning. He had time to kill.

He went to see a movie and sat through the main feature twice. Then he had supper in a cafeteria and went back to his room to wait.

The girl moved in around half past eleven the next morning. Eddie watched from his window and saw her taxi pull up, saw her get out, carrying a medium-sized suitcase, saw her come into the building. He waited, wondering if this was the messenger from the Syndicate. She was really a looker—around twenty-three or twenty-four, a willowy blonde with a long yellow ponytail dangling down her back.

She was wearing red pedal-pushers that clung tightly to the stunning curves of her hips and buttocks. Her breasts thrust steeply out of the print shirt she was wearing. Even from three stories up, the view was eye-opening.

A couple of minutes passed, and then Eddie heard footsteps coming past his door. They didn't stop. He couldn't resist a peek; he opened the door, peeped out, and saw the sensational blonde and the landlady disappearing into a room at the end of the hall. Eddie ducked back into his room and closed the door.

Not a messenger from the Syndicate at all. Just a new tenant. But he didn't mind that. In the next couple of days, he thought, maybe he could make some hay.

At twelve sharp he left his room and went out to get some lunch. The arrangement with the Syndicate always was that he would be allowed to leave his room from nine to ten, from twelve to one, and from six to seven.

The rest of the time he had to stay put and wait for the pickup to come. He walked up to Broadway and ate in the cafeteria where he was having all his meals, and broke another queer tenspot for a $1.25 lunch.

When he returned to the rooming house he noticed the ponytail girl walking a few paces in front of him. He quickened his speed and caught up with her.

Eddie liked to think he was a big man with the ladies. He pulled up alongside her and said, "Hello, neighbor."

She smiled. Close up, she was a knockout.

"Hello."

"We live on the same floor. I saw you move in this morning."

"Oh. Then we *are* neighbors."

They reached the rooming house and turned in. They walked up the stairs. Eddie made light talk with her, and he could see she liked him. His throat was dry with excitement. She was fabulously built—big high breasts, narrow waist, flaring hips. The legs revealed by the skin-tight pedal-pushers were flawless. Eddie wondered if she were some kind of starlet. She sure had a Hollywood figure. But what was she doing in a cheap dump like this, in that case?

She smiled at him and went on into her room. Eddie stood in the hallway, looking moonily after her until she had closed the door.

He hadn't had a woman in a long time. And he didn't even remember when he had had one like this. And something told him that this girl was available.

The Syndicate didn't like him fooling around with women while he was on a delivery trip. They wanted him to keep his mind on business, and nothing but.

But the Syndicate didn't have to know, did they? Eddie walked to the window and looked out. He wished the Syndicate would send its man over to pick up the plates. Then he could take himself a couple of days to make time with the blonde, before he went back to Chi.

*

The afternoon passed along, and Eddie fidgeted. He couldn't leave his room. And no one showed up.

Sometimes they waited, he thought. He remembered once in Seattle when the town was lousy with FBI men because of a kidnapping, and the Syndicate had been afraid to make the pickup until the heat died down. So Eddie had had to sit around for four whole days waiting for someone to come take the plates from him.

There was nothing he could do but wait. He couldn't get in touch with the Syndicate and say, "Come get them." He didn't even know the address, just the box number. So he paced around. At six o'clock nobody had shown up, and he went out to the cafeteria, returning around quarter to seven.

At five minutes to seven somebody knocked on Eddie's door.

He jumped up, stubbing his cigarette out. He looked at his watch and frowned. If it was the Syndicate man, he was five minutes early. And Syndicate men *never* came when they weren't supposed to.

He said, "Who is it?"

"Me. Joan."

It was the girl from down the hall. Cautiously, Eddie opened the door. She grinned up at him. She was still wearing the shirt and pedal-pushers, but she had the waist of the shirt out and tied in a knot just below her breasts, leaving her middle bare and emphasizing the contour of her figure.

She held up an unopened bottle of wine and said, "Hope I'm not disturbing you. I bought this bottle of wine and now I can't find my corkscrew. I was wondering if you had one."

Eddie smiled. "Happens I do," he said. "Little one, attached to my penknife." He couldn't keep his eyes off her body. Those big pointed breasts, those flaring hips, the thighs tightly encased in red cloth…

"That's swell," she said. "Say, are you doing anything for the next couple of hours?"

"Me? No, not much."

"I figure, as long as I've got the bottle and you've got the corkscrew, we could have a share-the-wealth arrangement. We can split the bottle and have a little party right up here."

His smile became broader, "That's a swell idea. Let's go down to your room and—"

"Oh, no," she said quickly. "My room's a mess. And it's much smaller than yours. We could stay here."

He frowned. He didn't like the idea of having a stranger in the same room as the plates. But what the hell: The plates were hidden away. And the girl was practically throwing herself at him. It was too good a bit to miss.

If the Syndicate man showed up, Eddie would stall him somehow. Chances were that nobody would come for the plates tonight. The Syndicate usually liked to make pickups of that sort in the daytime, for some reason.

"Okay," he said. "Go get a glass, and we'll have a little party."

*

She hustled down the hall, returning with a drinking glass. Eddie let her in and locked the door behind her. She handed him the bottle of wine, and he took out his penknife, which had half a dozen gadgets on it including a small corkscrew. It was a big knife, and he was proud of it. He stuck the screw into the cork, braced the bottle between his feet, and pulled.

The cork popped free.

"Bravo!" the girl said.

He poured out a glassful of the wine for her, and one for him. They drank.

Eddie sized her up. He had an idea about her, now; she was either a starlet or an heiress, but she was also a wino. She had a compulsion to live in cheap hotels and drink cheap wine and sleep with strange men. Eddie had heard of girls like that. Rich girls who wanted to sink into the slums. Well, he was willing to take all the fun he could from her.

Midway in the second glass of wine, she came over and sat down next to him on the bed. He put his arms around her and they kissed, and he set his glass down and cupped her full breasts, and ran the hand all over her body until he was tingling with desire. He prayed that no Syndicate man would show up now. The way it looked, this girl was good for all the way and back again.

But she wiggled away again when the caress started to get too passionate. Eddie looked a little hurt, and she said, "We don't want to rush things. We've got all night, Eddie-boy."

"Yeah. All night."

He drank some more wine. She picked up the knife, still lying on the night-table with the cork stuck in the corkscrew, and hefted it.

"Whew. This thing must weigh a pound."

"It's a good knife. Got all the gadgets. I picked it up in Germany right after the war."

Deftly she pulled the cork free and snapped the corkscrew back into hiding. Eddie watched her, smiling, as her delicate fingers tugged the biggest blade out. She wrapped her hand around the butt.

Then, suddenly, she put the blade to his belly.

He laughed. "Don't play games like that. It's dangerous."

"It's not a game, Eddie-boy." Her voice sounded different all of a sudden. She looked him straight in the eye and said, "Where are the plates, Eddie?"

The unexpected question hit him like a sledgehammer between the eyes. He tried to bluff out of it. "What you talking about, huh? Plates?"

"You know damn well what I mean. Plates for ten-dollar bills. You brought them all the way from Chicago to deliver them to the Syndicate."

"Are you from the Syndicate?"

She smiled. Evil flashed in her eyes. "The Los Angeles branch of the Syndicate has been taken over, Eddie. Different people are running the show now. They sent me to get the plates."

"I gotta have identification."

She nudged him with the knife. "Here's your identification, Eddie."

His mind struggled to fathom what was happening. The Syndicate taken over? How could that be? The Syndicate was too powerful for that.

Yet here was this girl who knew all about it, and she was holding his own knife in his ribs.

He said slowly, "Suppose I don't tell you where the plates are?"

"You'll tell me, Eddie."

He shrugged. "Suppose I don't. What then? It ain't gonna do you any good to stick me with that knife, is it? I won't tell you when I'm dead."

"You've got them right here in this room."

"You can't be sure of that. Maybe I've got them in a safety box somewhere. Maybe I've got them hidden so deep you'll never find them. Take the knife out of my ribs, girlie. You won't get the plates that way."

The pressure of the blade eased. She said, "We got ways of making you tell us where the plates are. We don't have to kill you all at once."

He shook his head. "You don't scare me." Then a crafty gleam came into his eyes. "There's only one quick easy way you can get the plates from me."

"What's that?"

"Buy them," he said.

The idea had sprung into his mind instantly. If someone could take over the Los Angeles branch of the Syndicate, that meant the Syndicate was sure to crumble everywhere else also. Which would leave him out of a job. So the smart thing to do was to get out right now. If he could get a nice price for the plates, he could duck across into Mexico and live a good life there. He had some money saved already, on deposit in a Mexican bank. He hadn't figured to quit the Syndicate for another ten years, but it looked like the smart thing to do was to get out right here and now with as much dough as he could salvage. Anyway, if he didn't give this girl the plates he was likely to get messed up but good.

She grinned coldly. "All right. Eddie. We won't torture you. Name your price for the plates."

"Ten thousand dollars," he said.

It was the first figure that leaped into his mind. He didn't have any idea how much the plates were really worth, but he figured ten g's was a good place to start the bargaining.

Only the girl didn't bargain. She nodded her head and said, "Okay, Eddie. You give us the plates and we'll give you ten grand. Then you clear out and forget you ever came to Los Angeles."

"When do I get the money?"

"Right now," she said. "You wait here. I'll go out into the hall and tell them to come over with it. Just sit tight."

Eddie sat. He heard the girl go out into the hall and drop a dime in the payphone out there. She dialed a number and someone answered and she said, "Yeah, he's got them. He's willing to sell out for ten grand and no questions asked. Bring the cash over here right away." She hung up.

When she came back in, Eddie said, "When did this takeover bit happen?"

"Last week. A couple of the guys near the bottom dumped the guys at the top and reorganized. We're not taking orders from Chi anymore, and we're not giving them a cut. But we have to have the plates. There's no engraver out here that can do the job."

Eddie nodded. "Okay. How about finishing what we started before?"

He reached out for her, but she stepped back and shook her head. "Not now. The guys will be here with the money in fifteen minutes."

"Fifteen minutes is plenty of time."

"Wait till they leave. Then we'll have all the time in the world," she promised.

Eddie smiled. This was turning out great. Ten thousand bucks in cash for the plates, and a spin in bed with this eye-popper too. And then tomorrow he'd pull out and head for Tijuana with his loot. The Chicago people would never be able to find him. Hell, they could get themselves a new courier. He'd been working this job long enough.

The minutes passed slowly. Finally a long black car pulled up in front of the house. Two men got out and went inside.

"There they are," the girl said.

A moment later, they were knocking on the door. Eddie let them in. They were big and ugly-looking.

"This the guy?" one of them asked.

"That's him," the girl said.

"Okay. Where's the plates?"

Eddie grinned and said, "Let's see the money. You give me the money and I'll give you the plates."

The smaller of the two men pulled a bulging black wallet out of his pocket and started to count out bills. Eddie got a close look and saw that they were hundred-dollar bills. He counted out ten, tidied them up, and started a new stack. By the time he was finished, there were ten neat little thousand-dollar stacks arranged on the table.

Eddie's mouth was watering. He picked up one of the bills and looked at it. It looked okay. They didn't print queer hundred-dollar bills, because it was too hard to pass them. Ten thousand bucks. He pushed the ten little stacks together with quivering hands and started to straighten the bills out.

"The plates," they reminded him.

"Oh. Yeah. Sure, the plates." Eddie gathered the money up and put the wine bottle on it as a paperweight. Then he went to his dresser drawer, reached under the shirts, pulled out the box. "It's locked," he said. "I don't have the key—the Syndicate men always had the key. But you can break it open to make sure it's the right stuff."

"We have the key," one of them told him. They opened the box and looked in. Eddie saw the gleaming copper plates. The box was closed.

He folded his arms. Now, as soon as the two goons cleared out, he and the girl could get down to some serious necking—

He realized suddenly that he was staring into the snouts of two silenced .38s.

"Hey," he said thinly. "What's the stunt? How come the guns?"

The girl laughed richly. "The joke's on you, Eddie. We *are* from the Syndicate. There hasn't been any change around here." She reached into the pocket of her pedal-pushers and took out a torn ten-dollar bill. She waved it at him. Eddie knew it matched the one he had in his wallet.

"I don't get it," he muttered. "Why—"

"It was all a little game, Eddie," she said, still smiling. "We wanted to see how loyal you were to the Syndicate. But you weren't very loyal, were you? You were in an awful hurry to sell out, it seems. So you aren't much good to us. The Chicago people said to test you, to make sure you were loyal." She shook her head. "Looks like you flunked the test, Eddie."

"No—wait—it was all a mistake!" he yelled. "I didn't really mean to sell the plates! I—"

One of the guns made a whining sound. Then the other one fired. Eddie felt the red-hot slugs rip into his body. He toppled forward, reaching out to the pile of hundred-dollar bills. The Syndicate mobsters fired again. Eddie's clutching hand pulled away from the bills, and he went sprawling forward onto the cheap rug, still trying to explain that it was all a mistake as Death took him.

ONE NIGHT OF VIOLENCE

It was past six in the evening when Mike Keller finished up the last stop of the day. By that time the sun was long since down, because it was a cold, chilly October day in central Wisconsin. Time to knock off for the day, Keller thought. He was a salesman, making the rounds for a furnace company. This was the first day of his regular three-day sales trip through the middle of the state.

He had covered a lot of ground that day, since he had started out bright and early in Fond du Lac. He was well into Columbia County, and the day had been pretty successful. Keller felt good about things, all factors considered. He enjoyed traveling around, talking to new people and getting to know them, getting them to like him and buy from him. And the job paid well. The only part about it that he didn't like was that he had to spend too much time away from Beth and the kids, making these long jaunts across Wisconsin and sleeping alone in cold, drafty motels instead of home with his wife.

But it was a good job, and after a few more years on the road they would give him a post in the home office, paying maybe ten or twelve thousand a year, and from then on everything would be swell.

Keller finished saying goodbye to his last customer of the day and climbed into his Oldsmobile. He hit the road, steaming along the flat, straight highway at an effortless 75 mph. His traveling schedule called for him to spend the night at a place called Wofford's Motel, on Route 16 near Wyocena. In the morning, he'd continue along Route 16, making some stops in Portage and Wisconsin Dells, then cutting south through Sauk County.

He stopped off at a roadhouse a few miles from the motel and ate a light supper, just some bean soup, frankfurters and beans, and coffee. When he was on the road, he usually ate his big meal at noontime. That gave him the extra energy to get through the day. When he was finished eating, he drove along the highway till he reached the turnoff that led to Wofford's Motel.

Usually, when he was on this route, he stopped at a place called Hickman's, two or three miles further along the road. But Hickman's tended to be a little stingy with the steam heat, and the rent was high. So a friend had suggested this other motel, Wofford's, and Keller decided to give it a try.

It looked just like a million other motels, when he drove up to it about quarter to eight that evening. It was one story high, a long rambling place spread out in the shape of a big letter "L," with a concrete motor-court filling in the middle. A dozen or so cars were parked in the motor-court, but the place didn't look anywhere near full.

Keller turned off the roadway, pulled his car into a vacant parking spot, and doused the motor. He took his small traveling suitcase from the back seat and trudged over to the neon-decorated doorway that said "OFFICE."

A tired-looking middle-aged man was sitting back of the desk reading a Milwaukee paper. He looked up at Keller without expression. "Yes?"

"I sent you a postcard last week, making a reservation for tonight. The name's Michael Keller."

Slowly, the desk man unlimbered himself and riffled through a reservation book. While he looked for Keller's card he said, "You sure didn't need to bother with a reservation tonight, fella. Damn if we have more than fifteen rooms full outa sixty."

Keller shrugged. "Guess I'm a cautious type, that's all. This time of year I like to *know* I got a room. I wouldn't want to have to go cruising around looking for one, late at night."

"Here we are," the clerk muttered, pulling Keller's card out of the book. "Okay. Room 23. Nine bucks for the night. That okay?"

Grinning, Keller said, "Nine bucks will *have* to be okay, won't it?" He took the key, picked up his suitcase, and headed across the paved walkway to the door numbered 23. He let himself in.

It wasn't a bad room at all—on the small side, but he didn't mind that. A single bed with a blue coverlet, a couple of chairs, a dresser, a neat little bathroom. There was a radio, but no television set. The room was nice and warm. Keller made a mental note to add this place to his list of good motels, for use whenever he happened to come through this section.

He unpacked and went through the little ritual of taking the framed photos of his wife and kids out and setting them up on the dresser. He did this wherever he went. He put his wife Beth's photo in the middle, surrounding it with the snaps of six-year-old Jeanie, four-year-old Tom, and Dannie, the baby.

Next thing he did was to take some motel stationery out of the dresser drawer. He wrote, as always, a postcard to Beth. He would mail it first thing in the morning at the next town he stopped at and she would get it the day after. He would be home late the night on which she received the postcard, but she always looked forward to the card anyway. He wrote simply that he had had a good day, hoped for equal good luck tomorrow, and that he sent his love to her and to the kids. He stuck a stamp on the postcard and set it aside.

He unpacked the book he was reading, took off his shoes, and sprawled in the armchair to read. One good thing about this job, he thought, was that he got time to do plenty of reading. For the first time in his life he could read some good books and improve himself. On this trip he was carrying a book by Zola. The last time out, it had been a book about the Revolutionary War.

The time was half past eight. Keller planned to read till about eleven, maybe eleven-thirty if he got really wrapped up in what he was reading. Then lights out, with the little alarm clock set for six-thirty ayem. Breakfast at seven, after a shower and a shave, and then, by eight, the first stop of the second day's route. He would make a big curving swing south through the Sac Prairie country, then start heading around on the homeward leg along Route 151 through Madison and back to Fond du Lac.

He started to get involved in the book, and time passed rapidly. Soon it was quarter after nine. Feeling thirsty, Keller laid the book aside and poured a drink of water for himself.

He heard the sound of a door slamming nearby. Then, footsteps and voices. The walls weren't very thick at this motel, apparently. He could hear the muffled sound of people speaking.

Then he heard something else. A woman's voice—she was screaming. The scream was cut short abruptly. It was as if a hand had been clapped suddenly over her mouth.

Keller frowned. *It's none of my business*, he told himself. He was a married man with three kids. It didn't make sense to butt into somebody else's quarrel.

But still, he was right next door. Maybe someone was getting hurt. He put his shoes on and went outside.

He paused for a second outside the adjoining room, Room 24, trying to make up his mind. He could hear a couple of low masculine voices inside, and a steady quiet female sobbing sound. The sensible thing would be to turn around and go back into his own room and forget the whole thing. Or else to phone the desk clerk and let *him* go investigate the scream.

But almost before he knew what he was doing, Keller reached out and knocked at the door of Room 24.

The door opened almost instantly. A lean-faced man with piercing eyes glared out at Keller. The man was about Keller's own height, five feet ten inches.

"Yeah? What is it?"

"Pardon me for intruding," Keller said mildly. "I'm in the room next door. I heard someone cry out, a couple of minutes ago, and I wondered if there was any way I could help—"

"Yeah," said the lean-faced man. He grinned, showing wolfish yellow teeth. "You *could* help out. Yeah."

Suddenly he reached out and caught Keller by the collar of his shirt. He yanked the salesman into the room with one quick jerk. Keller was too surprised to do anything but tumble inward.

The door slammed shut behind him and he heard the lock click. In his first puzzled moment he looked around at the group that faced him.

He saw the gun first. He knew enough about guns to recognize it was a .357 Magnum that, at this distance, could blow a hole through him big enough to fit a cat through.

The man holding the gun was sitting in the armchair, legs crossed. He was a pudgy-looking, greasy-faced man with glossy black hair.

The girl was on the bed. She was a blonde, in her early twenties. She was wearing only a brassiere and a slip. She had been tied up with strips torn from her dress and her blouse, and one side of her face was puffing up where someone had hit her.

The lean-faced man was standing by the door. There

was a third man in the room, a good-looking fair-haired kid of about twenty or twenty-one. He was sitting on the bed, ready to clap his hand over the girl's mouth if she tried to yell again.

Keller felt his knees go watery. He was thirty-four, so he had been old enough to be drafted in World War II, but he had spent the whole war policing a prisoner-of-war camp in Colorado, and this was the first time in his life anyone had ever pointed a gun at him and meant it. He wanted to sit down, but there was no place to sit.

He said, "Look here, guys, I don't want any trouble. I don't know what you're up to, but I'm a married man with kids and I want out."

"Shut up," said the man with the gun.

"I'll go back to my room and forget I ever came in here," Keller pleaded. "I don't want to get mixed up in—"

"Shut up," said the man with the gun a second time. The big gun twitched meaningfully in a little circle and came to rest in a dead line with Keller's forehead. Keller gulped and decided not to say anything further just now. The girl on the bed was staring at him oddly, almost with sympathy. Keller wondered what this caper was all about. He wished fervently that he had minded his own business and not tried to play Boy Scout.

"Raise your hands high up in the air," the fat man with the gun commanded thinly.

Keller obeyed without a word. The hard-looking man who had pulled him inside approached him and efficiently frisked him from shoulders to hips.

"He's clean," the hard-faced man reported.

"Good," the fat man commented. He stared at Keller.

"Okay. When you stuck your face in here a minute ago, you asked if you could help. Well, the answer is yes. You can help us quite a bit."

Keller stood stiffly erect, feeling tremendously uncomfortable. He thought of his book lying face down in his own room, only a few feet away. He thought of Beth, many miles to the east. By now all the children would be asleep. Beth would be in the living room, listening to the radio, sewing, maybe. Perhaps Nora Matthews from next door had come to visit her. Certainly Beth was not at all likely to suspect that at this moment her husband was looking down the barrel of a deadly .357 Magnum.

"How can I help you?" Keller asked.

"You know what a Judas goat is?" asked the plump, greasy-faced man.

Keller nodded jerkily. "The Judas goat is the one that leads the rest of the herd to slaughter," he said in an uneven voice.

"Yeah. That's right. Well, we want you to be our Judas goat for us. It's nice and convenient that you dropped in just when you did. Saved us the trouble of looking around for a fellow to help us out."

"Just what do you want me to do?" Keller asked. "Who are you, anyway? What's going on here?"

The greasy-faced man said, "My name is Johnny Coppola. Does that mean anything to you?"

"No. Should it?"

"Depends on how law-abiding you are," Coppola said.

"Plenty," Keller said.

"Then you ain't likely to know me. But everyone in Chicago does. I've got a few—uh—business enterprises down in Chicago. These men are two of my associates. Three more of my associates are registered in other rooms of this motel."

Chicago gangsters, Keller said to himself. His throat was terribly dry.

"As for the girl," Coppola went on, "her name happens to be Peggy Ryan. She keeps company with a cheap hood name of Mike Fitzpatrick. You know Fitzpatrick?"

Keller shook his head.

Coppola shrugged. "Fitzpatrick is also a Chicago operator. But he happens to be up in this neighborhood right now, because two days ago someone kidnapped his girlfriend Peggy and someone else sent him an anonymous tip that she had been taken up into middle Wisconsin."

Keller looked at the girl on the bed. Her hands were tied behind her back, and her ankles were tied together. Her face was full, her lips moist and sensual. Hatred smoldered in her eyes. She had high round breasts and long, creamy legs.

Coppola said, "Fitzpatrick is looking for his girlfriend and he wants her back real hard. He and his boys are in a hotel in Portage, a few miles up the road. And here's where you come in. We sort of want you to drive up to Portage and find Mike Fitzpatrick, and tell him where his girlfriend is. Tell him that she was abandoned by her kidnappers and that she wants him to come pick her up. That's all you have to do."

"And then what happens?"

"To you, nothing. You go away and forget you ever came here tonight."

"But to Mike Fitzpatrick? It's a trap for him, isn't it?" Keller asked. "I lure him down here with the girl as bait, and he comes in here all unsuspecting—"

"Yeah," said the hard-faced man behind him. "You sort of get the picture fast, smart boy."

Keller nodded. He didn't give a damn if these two mobs slaughtered each other. He just wanted to get out of here, away from that cannon pointed at him, wanted to get away alive and without any holes in him.

"Okay," Keller said. "I'll do whatever you want me to if you'll leave me alone afterward. You want me to go right now?"

Coppola nodded. "Yeah. You have a car, don't you?"

"Yes," Keller said.

"Okay. You get in your car and go up to Portage. He's at the Bailey Hotel. You tell him that Peggy Ryan is down here at—what's the name of this place—Wofford's. You tell him that she was kidnapped, but her heisters got scared off when they learned that he was in the next town, and they dropped her at this motel. You tell him that she's stuck at the motel without a dime, and the motel owner won't let her check out and he's watching her like a hawk, and so he has to come down in person to her. And you give him this, just as a clincher."

Coppola nodded and the hard-faced man handed Keller a ring. It was a diamond ring, about two carats. Keller looked at it closely. It was inscribed along the inside of the band, *To Peggy from Mike, with all my love.* Keller guessed that a ring like this might be worth a couple of thousand.

"Everything clear?" Coppola asked.

Keller nodded. "I'll leave right away."

The fat gangster grinned. "Just one more little thing. Gimme your wallet."

"My wallet? But—"

Keller felt the hard-faced man prod him in the ribs. He took his wallet out and handed it to Coppola. He had about eighty bucks in it, but Coppola obviously wasn't interested in the cash. He was looking through the wallet, through the card section and the photos. Keller kept snapshots of Beth and the kids in the wallet.

Finally Coppola looked up, smiling coldly. He drew Keller's social-security card from the wallet and handed everything else back to Keller. He said, "Okay Mr. Mike Keller of 404 Maple Avenue, Fond du Lac, Wisconsin. I see you got a wife and three kids. That's nice."

"What are you getting at?" Keller asked edgily.

"I just want some insurance. I want to make sure you won't just get away and never come back. And I want to make sure you don't louse us up by tipping off Fitzpatrick."

"I won't try any funny stuff," Keller promised.

"You better not. Because in case you never go to Fitzpatrick, or in case you call the cops, or in case you pull some other stunt—if you try any of that, Mr. Mike Keller, and anybody in my gang should survive this night, you're going to regret it. I know where you live, now. I know you got a family. And if you try to cross me, Keller, I'll see to it that you and your family get hunted down and wiped out, one by one. First your kids and then your wife, and you last of all. You got that straight?"

"Don't worry. I won't cross you." Keller's voice was hoarse-sounding He was no more of a coward than the next guy. But this kind of threat shook him deeply.

"Good," Coppola said "Okay. Scram. Bailey's Hotel, in Portage. And remember my warning."

The hard-faced man opened the door for him, and Keller stepped out onto the little porch that ran the whole length of the motel. He gripped the railing tight and took a deep breath. His heart was thundering.

He knew he didn't have any choice but to do what Coppola wanted. It was too risky to try calling the mobster's bluff. He couldn't risk the lives of Beth and the kids by notifying the police or by simply leaving the motel and vanishing. Maybe Coppola would track him down and maybe not, but there was no sense chancing it.

Keller let himself into his own room and slipped into his jacket. His book still lay where he had put it down, twenty minutes ago. He shook his head mournfully. If he hadn't butted in where he didn't belong, he wouldn't be caught up in this pattern of violence and revenge now.

But it was no good trying to second-guess. He *had* butted in, and now he was forced to be an unwilling accomplice in the ambush Johnny Coppola was planning for his gang enemy.

He took his car keys from the dresser, locked up his room, and went outside again, down the porch steps and toward his car. He saw that the door of Room 24 was slightly ajar. Although he could see no one, he was certain that the lean, hard-faced man was standing there, peering out, watching him.

Keller got behind the wheel of his car. His hand was shaking so much that he had trouble fitting the key into the ignition. But finally he got the car moving, and drove down the motel driveway and onto the main road, heading north and west toward the town of Portage.

It was no more than five miles away—a six- or seven-minute drive, at best. The night was quietly cold, with an almost-full moon lighting up the broad flat countryside, and a sharp sprinkling of stars overhead. The time was about quarter to ten. Back home, Beth would probably be combing out her long, lovely red-brown hair now, and getting ready for bed. He missed her tremendously.

While he was still a couple of miles from Portage, he drove up to a late-night roadhouse whose neon signs proclaimed BEER WINE WHISKEY COCKTAILS. The place was full of local kids, rocking and rolling to the strains of a booming jukebox. Keller steadied his nerves with a single shot of bourbon, then returned to the car. Ordinarily he did not drink while he was behind the wheel, but tonight, he thought, was something special. One shot wouldn't affect his coordination much, and it would go a long way to settle the butterflies in his stomach.

A few minutes later he was in Portage, a town of about eight thousand people. He had been through the town maybe fifty times in the last few years, but he had never stayed in it overnight, and so he had no idea where the Bailey Hotel was. He pulled up at a gas station.

When the serviceman came out, Keller said, "I'm looking for the Bailey Hotel."

"Go along Main for a while, then turn left at the third traffic light. The Bailey's on the left-hand side of the street. You can't miss it."

"Thanks. Let me have three bucks' worth in the tank, too, while you're at it."

While the station-man filled the gas tank, Keller jotted the amount down on his expense card with a shaky hand. The man grinned at him as Keller forked over three singles.

"Say, Mac, are you feeling okay?"

"Sure," Keller said.

"Well, you look kinda pale to me, that's all."

"Just nerves," Keller said. "Been working a rough schedule. You know how it is."

"Yeah. Well, take it easy."

Keller drove off. Not much later, he reached the third traffic light on Main, turned left, and pulled his car to a halt outside the swinging sign that read BAILEY HOTEL.

It was a dingy-looking place, four stories high, with a red-brick front. Keller went inside.

It had the usual kind of cheap-hotel lobby—old battered armchairs, a couple of tables covered with last month's magazines, a video set, a few big potted plants in the corners. The man at the desk was playing solitaire when Keller came up to him.

"I'm looking for a party named Fitzpatrick, from Chicago. Could you give me the room?"

The desk clerk frowned "Don't think, we have any Fitzpatricks here. Lemme check."

He checked. When he was through checking, he shook his head. "Sorry, nobody by that name been here all week. Maybe at Crawford's, four blocks up—"

Keller shook his head. "Maybe Fitzpatrick isn't here yet," he said. He should have realized that the gangster would not have registered under his own name. "But some of his friends must have arrived. You have anyone else from Chicago here?" Keller took a wild flyer. "Mr. Smith, maybe, or Mr. Jones?"

The clerk brightened. "Yeah. Room 34, upstairs—here it is, Smith and two friends, all from Chicago. I'll ring them and find out if they're in. Who's calling, please?"

Keller said, "Tell them it's Mr. Black. Tell them I'm a friend of Miss Ryan."

"Okay. Hold on." The clerk ambled over to the switchboard, plugged in a jack, and waited. A moment later he said, "Mr. Smith? The desk calling. A gentleman named Mr. Black is here, says he wants to see you. He says he's a friend of Miss Ryan. Yeah, that's right. Ryan." There was a long pause. "He'll be right up," the clerk said, and broke the connection. He said to Keller, "Take the elevator over there. It's on the third floor."

The elevator was an old creaky affair that wheezed and moaned all the way up. Keller was glad to get out of it on the third floor.

Room 34 was right opposite the elevator. Keller knocked once and the door opened. He found himself facing a man in his early thirties, with sharp cheekbones and an ugly scar lacing diagonally across one cheek. Behind him were two other men, one heavyset and muscular, the other smaller and thinner. The air of the room was gray with cigarette smoke.

The one with the cheekbones said, "I'm Mr. Smith. You want to see me?"

"I have a message from Miss Ryan," Keller said, trying to keep his voice calm. "Can I come in?"

"Sure," the man who called himself Smith said. Keller stepped inside. He noticed that all three men were poised, ready to whip out guns at the first hint of trouble. Well, he wasn't going to make any trouble.

He had already taken the diamond ring out and held it in the palm of his hand, so it would not be necessary for him to reach into his pockets and so possibly draw fire. He opened his hand and held the ring out.

"Does this look familiar, Mr. Smith?"

Smith's hard eyes glared. "Where did you get that ring?" he demanded.

"Miss Ryan gave it to me to bring to you. That is, if your name isn't Smith. She said the man I was looking for was named Fitzpatrick. Is that you?"

"Maybe," Smith said. "But suppose you start telling me things, and tell them fast. What do you want? Why did she give you the ring? Who the hell are you, anyway?"

"I'm just an innocent bystander," Keller said. "I'm a furnace salesman, and I pulled into this motel tonight, and ten minutes after I got settled in my room there was a knock on the door. A girl. Blonde, young. Scared looking. She told me she'd been kidnapped by some gangsters in Chicago a couple of days ago and taken up here. That her boyfriend and his pals were on her trail. The kidnappers had found out they were being traced, and they left her at the motel and beat it. She said her boyfriend's name was Mike Fitzpatrick, and he was staying at the Bailey Hotel in Portage, and she asked me to drive up there and take a message to him for her."

"Why couldn't you just drive her up here, instead of all this roundabout business?"

"She owes two days' rent at the motel," Keller said. "The owner won't listen to any stories about kidnapping. He keeps an eye on her and won't let her off the grounds for fear she'll skip. But it was okay for her to send me out and have me tell you to come get her. That's why she gave me this ring, so you'd believe me."

Keller handed the ring to "Smith," who looked at it once, then fingered it without looking at it. "Okay," the man who called himself Smith said. "You came to the right guy. I'm Mike Fitzpatrick. These are some friends of mine. Where's the motel?"

"Down near Wyocena, on Route 16. The name of the place is Wofford's."

"And Peggy's down there?"

"Yeah. In Room 24."

"Okay," Mike Fitzpatrick said. "Let's get going, then. Wofford's Motel, on Route 16. Come on."

They went downstairs, the four of them—Fitzpatrick, his two fellow thugs, and Keller. Fitzpatrick's car was out in front of the hotel—a long, slow, sleek sedan, with Illinois license plates. The car made Keller's auto, which was two years old, look like a venerable heap.

"You drive ahead," Fitzpatrick ordered. "We'll follow along behind you."

"Okay," Keller said nervously.

He got into his own car and started it, driving back through the quiet streets of the town toward the highway. He saw the low black sedan in his rear-view mirror, keeping twenty or thirty feet behind him. His hands gripped the wheel tightly. It was all like something out of a nightmare, he thought. Kidnappings, gangland vendettas, black sedans with Illinois plates.

His mind's eye leaped ahead fifteen minutes or so, to the arrival at the motel. He could see it all clearly—Fitzpatrick and his men going up to Room 24, knocking on the door; then the door opening, the sudden unexpected blaze of gunfire, Fitzpatrick falling in a bloody heap while Coppola and his gang raced for their cars and made a getaway.

On the other hand, he pictured what would happen if through some miracle Fitzpatrick or one of his men escaped the lead fury. Certainly they would kill him, for having decoyed them into the trap. They would not care that he had had no choice; all that interested them was the fact that the salesman had led them into a deathtrap.

Keller's jaws tightened. His face was a pale, sweating mask. Desperately, he wanted out. He desired no part in the violence yet to come. He wanted to be a dozen miles away when the first explosions of gunfire began.

In no time at all, they were approaching Wofford's Motel. Keller glanced at his watch. Almost eleven o'clock. The few miles between the motel and Portage had slipped by too fast. Now they were here. Now it was time for the showdown. A new thought occurred.

Suppose Coppola opened fire the moment Fitzpatrick stepped from his car? Keller was sure to get caught in the middle, that way. Bullets would be flying in every direction. It was not safe to enter the motel's parking court. Perhaps Coppola intended to kill him, too, just to eradicate the one witness who might be able to help the police untangle the night's violence.

He made up his mind. He slowed his car to a halt while he was still a hundred yards from the entrance to the motel. He yanked back the handbrake and got out. Fitzpatrick's car had stopped not far behind his. Keller walked over to the parked sedan.

Fitzpatrick was sitting in front, next to the driver. He unrolled his window and looked out. The gangster's face was shiny with sweat. Evidently Fitzpatrick was suspicious of a trap.

"What's going on?" the mobster demanded. "How come you stopped out here on the road?"

"The motel's right in front of us," Keller said. "You go on around me and drive in. I'm gonna go up the road for a cup of coffee before I go in."

"Like hell you are, bud," Fitzpatrick snapped. "You ain't going for any cups of coffee right now."

"Huh? Look here—"

"*You* look here. How much does the girl owe the management for two days' rent?"

Keller was startled by the question. He stammered for a moment before saying, "Oh, eighteen or nineteen bucks, I guess."

"Good." Fitzpatrick peeled two crisp new ten-dollar bills from a thick roll. "This ought to cover it, then. Here. Give her the dough and tell her we're waiting up the road for her."

Keller stared at the two bills in his hand. He hadn't expected Fitzpatrick to pull something like this.

"Why can't *you* go in there and check her out?" Keller asked.

Fitzpatrick smiled coldly. "These days I don't go walking in nowhere without a couple of affidavits first. How do I know this ain't some kind of trap?"

Keller tongued his dry lips.

How right you are! he thought silently. But what did he do now? He couldn't possibly produce the girl.

"Whatsamatter?" Fitzpatrick demanded roughly, when Keller remained silent. "There *is* funny business going on here, ain't there? Ain't there?"

"No funny business," Keller said thinly. "The girl sent me to get you."

"Okay, then bring her out here."

Keller nodded helplessly. An idea struck him. He walked away, down the hundred yards of road and into the motel court. He stood behind some shrubbery for a couple of minutes, then walked out again and back to Fitzpatrick's car.

"Well?"

"She won't come," Keller said. "She says she's afraid to trust anybody. You have to go in there and get her yourself."

Without a word, Fitzpatrick got out of his car, slamming the door hard. He walked over to Keller. With a lightning-fast motion he got one hand clamped around Keller's throat and shook him.

Keller made no attempt to defend himself. Not against three men with guns. He sputtered and tried to breathe.

Fitzpatrick grated, "It's a trap, ain't it? Coppola's holed up there with Peggy, and he's waiting for me to come waltzing in and get cooled. Well, I'm just as smart as he is, and maybe a little smarter! Answer me! Is it a trap or isn't it?"

Keller made a strangling sound. Fitzpatrick released

him, and Keller gasped for breath. After a minute he said, "Don't know what you're talking about—traps—girl asked me to drive up to Portage and—"

Fitzpatrick slapped him hard, backhand. Blood began to well from a split corner of Keller's lower lip. The gangster said after a moment, "All right, wise guy. We'll see whether it's a trap or not. *You're* going to spring it."

"I'm telling you—"

"Shut up. Come on. We'll all go walk into that motel court. You can lead the way. You can walk up to Room 24 and knock on the door. Then the door opens. If it's a trap, *you're* the first one who gets shot." Fitzgerald gestured with his thumb. "Let's go."

The hundred yards seemed to take forever. Keller's legs longed to fold up under him.

He knew what would happen as soon as he entered the main plaza of the motor-court leading the three gangsters. Coppola's men would open fire. He would be cut down along with Fitzpatrick and the others. Fitzpatrick was counting on having Keller crack before they reached the entrance. Fitzpatrick was right. Ten yards still remained when Keller said, "Hold it," and stopped.

"You want to tell us something?" Fitzpatrick asked.

"Yeah," Keller said, breathing heavily. "I don't have anything to do with this. I'm just a guy who checked into the motel tonight. But you guessed right—it *is* a trap. Coppola and two other guys are in Room 24 with your girl. I guess the idea is to gun you down when you go to

get her. They said they'd kill my wife and children if I
didn't decoy you into it."

Fitzpatrick's smile was ugly. "Good thing you wised up
and told us in time, pal. This switches things around a
whole lot."

He glanced at one of his companions. "Get some rope
from the car, Sammy."

The heavyset thug jogged back to the sedan, opened
the trunk, and took out a coil of hemp. Returning, he and
his comrade quickly trussed Keller's legs together, then
his arms, while Fitzpatrick supervised.

"This is just to keep you out of trouble for a while,"
Fitzpatrick explained. "And so we can find you again later
if you've pulled some kind of triple-cross on us. So long,
sucker."

Keller lay by the side of the road, a hundred yards from
his own car, unable to move, and watched the three gangsters stealthily move toward the entrance of Wofford's
Motel. The furnace salesman was bathed in his own per-
spiration by now. Thoughts spun wildly through his mind,
as he figured all the possibilities and tried to compute the
way they would affect him.

No doubt Fitzpatrick and his men would try some kind
of sneak assault on Room 24. Keller figured the different
things that might happen. If Fitzpatrick and his two fellow
hoods succeeded in killing the Coppola outfit, they might
still come back here and kill him too, just to silence him.
But if Coppola emerged the victor, he would probably go

after Keller for having betrayed him—or even just to shut him up.

Either way, Keller realized coldly, he was a dead man. Whether Fitzpatrick's side won the duel or Coppola's. His only hope was that all of them get killed. Every last one. Only then would he be safe.

The road was utterly silent. No cars were coming by—not now, after eleven o'clock. Keller wondered what Fitzpatrick planned to do. Duck around back, perhaps. Or try to lure Coppola into the open.

He momentarily stopped conjecturing and fought with his bonds. They were well tied; they sliced painfully into his wrists and ankles. But he knew a little about knots. And he had strong fingers. He struggled to maneuver himself into a position where he could go to work on the ropes.

There, he thought, bending and twisting backward. His clutching fingers managed to snag the ropes binding his ankles. It was difficult work. A chill wind roared down on him. In the forty-degree weather, his hands were growing numb rapidly.

But he had an end of the rope, now, and he deftly twisted and maneuvered. He had to get free, he told himself. *Had* to. For Beth and the kids.

The rope gave momentarily in his hands. He took up the slack, weaved it through a loop, and suddenly he realized that he was going to get his legs free. The knot was open. It was just a matter of unwinding the tight cord, now. Around and around and around, and abruptly he could move his legs again. He paused for a moment, letting the circulation return. Then, bracing himself against a tree, he clambered to a standing position.

Hands, now. That was a tougher proposition. His wrists were pinioned behind his back, and it was impossible for him to reach the cord with his fingers. He looked around, hoping to find something he could use to sever the cord with. Rub it against a tree trunk? That might take forever before the friction weakened the rope. But there had to be some way. He had to get free. His heart pounded mercilessly. Five minutes had passed since the Fitzpatrick outfit had entered the motel grounds. What was happening? Why was it so silent?

The car, Keller thought in sudden triumph.

Fitzpatrick's sedan was parked just behind his own car. Breathless, Keller ran to it. It was as he thought. The sleek sedan sported a hood ornament—a streamlined torpedo shape that came to a sharp point!

Keller approached the mobster's car back-first. He put his feet on the bumpers and stood up, leaning back, so his wrists faced the sharp hood ornament. He set to work, digging the point of the ornament between the fibers of the rope, ripping, weakening. It was tough work. But he kept at it, twisting and pulling and once almost toppling face-forward off the bumpers.

And finally the frayed rope snapped.

Keller whipped his arms apart. Feverishly he undid the knots, ripped off the fragments of rope, freed himself. He rubbed his aching hands together. He was free!

His first thought was to get into his car and drive away. Far away, maybe even home to Beth. He could always come back some other time to pick up his belongings from the motel owner.

But a moment later he realized with strange clarity that to run away now was the worst thing he could do. He had to stay here and find out what happened. He had to make sure none of Coppola's gang escaped to make good their threat against him and against his family. He had to make sure none of Fitzpatrick's men escaped to carry out vengeance against him. He could not run away now. If he did, he would live in lingering fear, never knowing when violence would enter his life once again.

He stood there, thinking things through. Suddenly a single shot split the silence of the night. Keller frowned.

Then, cautiously, he began to make his way toward the entrance to Wofford's Motel.

Two more shots—and a man's scream—shattered the night before Keller reached the entrance. He paused for a moment at the arched neon gateway to the motel. For the second time tonight he was sticking his neck out when it was safer just to remain hidden away like a turtle in its shell.

But this time he had to know what was happening.

He ducked around the gateway and peered into the long L-shaped court of the motel. Lights were on all over the place, but no one was coming out of his room to investigate the shooting.

Keller glanced up at Room 24. The front window, he saw, had been splintered by a bullet.

Suddenly bright bursts of light spurted from the facing wing of the L. Keller ducked instinctively, but the shots were not aimed for him. He realized that Fitzpatrick's men were lying in the courtyard, concealed behind two of the parked cars. From where he stood he could see them plainly—the heavyset one named Sammy, and the thin, short one. Fitzpatrick was nowhere to be seen. His two henchmen lay behind the cars, sighting over their hoods and pumping shots through the window of Room 24. All the way across the court, on the facing wing of the L, they were drawing fire from two men Keller had never seen before. He realized that these must be other confederates of Coppola. He remembered that Coppola had said that three more "associates" of his were registered in other rooms of the motel.

Then he saw the third "associate." There was a man sprawled grotesquely out in a pool of blood, almost at the feet of the two Coppola thugs at the far side of the motor court. So one of the pudgy gangster's men was dead or seriously wounded already. That left five, including Coppola himself, to fight off three attackers. That is, if Fitzpatrick were still alive.

From his vantage point near the entrance to the motel, Keller watched the thin Fitzpatrick man edging through the side of the motor-court while the bigger one covered him. Suddenly Keller heard shots from a distance, muffled-sounding.

He knew where Fitzpatrick was. The scar-faced man had gone around back of the motel, and was firing into the rear window of Room 24. Another scream told him that a second Coppola man had been hit. The men in Room 24 were under attack from both front and rear, now.

But the two men at the far end of the L were preventing any careful assault from the front, because they were keeping up a more or less constant fire.

Keller wondered about the girl in the room under fire. Probably she was locked in the bathroom and out of danger. But was Fitzpatrick so anxious to kill Coppola that he was willing to risk hitting the girl? Evidently he was, Keller realized.

There was another exchange of shots. One went astray and smashed into the window of Room 23, Keller's room. He grinned despite himself. It was a lucky thing he was somewhere else, he told himself.

For two or three minutes after that exchange, there was silence. By this time, Keller thought, the motel proprietor had probably notified the police of the gun battle. But it would take time for the cops to arrive—maybe as much as ten or fifteen minutes, if they were coming from Portage, the nearest good-sized town. Plenty could happen in ten or fifteen minutes.

Keller noticed that the thin man was still creeping toward the porch, despite an occasional burst from the two strafers on the other wing of the motel. A sudden loud interchange of shots took place and one of the two

Coppola men uttered a horrible gargling scream and dropped forward onto the concrete parking area.

Two Coppola men down now. The remaining man out there huddled behind a stanchion and pumped a fruitless shot toward the two Fitzpatrick men. The odds were narrowing, now. Four against three.

But where was Fitzpatrick?

Keller heard a sudden voice.

Coppola's. "Fitzpatrick, can you hear me? Call off your men or I'll kill the girl! I'll kill her!"

Silence.

Then, out of nowhere, the sound of shattering glass, followed by a howl of rage.

Smoke began to pour from the front window of Room 24. A curious greenish greasy smoke.

Keller realized why Fitzpatrick had been silent so long. The gangster had obviously taken the opportunity to slip around back through the dark woods, past the motel grounds, back to his car. He had taken some sort of gas bomb out and, returning, hurled it through the rear window of Room 24.

Coppola was smoked out! Keller heard choking, coughing sounds. Smoke still billowed through the broken window. He wondered how long Coppola and his two henchmen could remain in the room.

He got his answer a moment later. The door of Room 24 was flung open. The youthful blond boy Keller had seen with Coppola earlier emerged. Blood already streaked his white shirt, and Keller realized that he was the one who had been wounded before. Now he came out coughing and screaming, with a gun in his right hand and his left arm thrown over his eyes.

The thin Fitzpatrick man sprang up immediately and fired two shots. The blond boy grabbed at his middle as a spout of red suddenly burst forth. He toppled forward, tumbling over the low railing and dropping with a heavy thud onto the hood of somebody's parked car.

But in the same instant the gun of the remaining Coppola mobster across the motor-court spoke. This time his aim was accurate. The thin man fell, yelling.

Keller revised his score. There were still two men in the room, Coppola and the hard-faced man, along with the girl. A third Coppola man was dug in for sniping across the way. Fitzpatrick was someplace in the back of the motel, and the heavyset man named Sammy was stationed out in front, behind a parked car.

Three against two. But it could only be a few more seconds before the smoke bomb forced Coppola and has aide out of Room 24. And in only a few more minutes the police would be here to mop up the survivors.

Fitzpatrick had appeared now. He came suddenly around the other side of the motel, rounding the L no more than fifty feet from Keller. But he did not even see Keller. The gangster took careful aim and blew the head off Coppola's sniper.

Two against two. And Fitzpatrick and Sammy were still fresh, while the two men in the room were struggling against the effects of a gas bomb.

The door of Room 24 opened a second time. Keller, crouching in the shadows, stared. The girl emerged this time.

She was nude. The brightness of the almost-full moon showed her pale, lovely body, and showed the tear-stained puffiness of her face. She came stumbling out of the room as if she had been pushed.

Keller saw Fitzpatrick go racing across the motor-court toward her. It was a mistake. Abruptly fat Coppola himself came from the room. He was wearing an improvised gas mask made out of strips of cloth, evidently torn from the girl's clothes.

Coppola chuckled harshly. Fitzpatrick was caught in the middle of the motor-court, with no place to hide. He had never expected Coppola to have been able to withstand the gassing, it seemed.

Coppola was holding the big .357 Magnum. He brushed aside the gauze that had protected his eyes and face and fired twice, in rapid succession.

The first shot caught Fitzpatrick square in the chest. The impact of the big slug ripping into him knocked the scar-faced man back almost ten feet. Fitzpatrick let out a grotesque howl and shrank into a crumpled dead heap. His gun went skittering out of his hands and came to rest no more than five paces from where Keller was hiding.

Coppola's second shot was aimed at Fitzpatrick's fleshy henchman, Sammy. But this time Coppola was not quite so lucky. The girl, Peggy Ryan, running wildly and blindly around the motor-court area, lurched in her hysterical flight and crossed in front of Coppola the instant his bullet was released.

Keller gasped. The .357 slug entered the girl's body between her shoulder blades and ripped its way right through her. A fountain of blood erupted between her full, ripe breasts. She stood transfixed, a white statue stained with red, frozen in the moonlight for a fraction of a second. Then the force of the shot knocked her down.

Sammy, who had been spared by her lucky lurch, made the most of his opportunity. He rose from his hiding place behind the car and pumped two slugs into Coppola's flabby body. The mob boss looked astonished and amazed. Coppola still had not fully realized that he had killed the girl instead of his remaining enemy. He frowned in a curious fashion, then clutched at his stomach and started to sag. Sammy tried to fire again at the falling Coppola, but his gun clicked and refused to deliver a shot. He had fired his last round.

Smoke had just about ceased to billow from Room 24 now. The gas bomb had spent itself. Sammy rose from hiding and looked around cautiously in all directions. Keller drew his breath in sharply as he saw the snout of a gun project from the glassless window of Room 24. Sammy had underestimated the number of his opponents. There was one left, the lean, hard-faced man who was the dead Coppola's second-in-command.

The gun in the window chattered three times.

Sammy whirled as the slugs thudded into him.

"What the—"

He never finished the sentence. He went down as though his legs had instantly turned to spaghetti. The motor-court was very silent. It was the silence of the tomb.

Keller, huddled up in the dark shrubbery near the entrance, felt some of the tension ebb out of him. The duel was over. They were all dead—Fitzpatrick, Sammy, the girl, Fitzpatrick's other thug, Coppola and the blond boy and the three others.

There had been only one survivor. The hard-faced man.

Keller shifted his feet. He was getting cramped. He looked out across the shambles that the pleasant little motel had become. Three dead men lay sprawled on the base of the L, over to his right. Closer to him lay the ugly corpse of Fitzpatrick. On the balcony was Coppola's body. Here and there in the parking area lay the corpses of Fitzpatrick's two henchmen, the girl, and the young blond-haired boy.

But there had been one survivor. Keller stared with new horror as he understood the full implication.

As he watched, the door of Room 24 swung slowly open for the last time. The hard-faced man came out. He looked in all directions. He had no way of knowing how many henchmen Fitzpatrick had come with.

But there was no sign of anyone else. Keller watched as the lean, cold-expressioned killer began to tiptoe across the balcony to the stairway, down to the parking area. He was going to drive away, now, before the police arrived.

The motel walls were cracked with bullet holes, and half a dozen windows had been smashed during the violent battle. No doubt the other guests had remained huddled under their beds all the while, not daring to look out. In only a minute or two, the police would probably show up.

Maybe, thought Keller, the police would get here in time to apprehend the hard-faced man.

Maybe not, though.

His mind dwelled for a moment on what might happen if the hard-faced man escaped. No doubt there were other members of the Coppola organization still in Chicago. They would want revenge. The hard-faced man would tell them of the furnace salesman who had tipped Fitzpatrick off about the ambush, and so caused the deaths of so many men.

They'll come after me, Keller thought. *They'll kill Beth and Jeanie and Tom and the baby, and me last of all.*

He could not let the hard-faced man escape.

Keller stood frozen in an agony of indecision. He was a law-abiding man. He knew how to use a gun, but he had never shot at any living thing in his life. And he knew that if he let that coldblooded killer escape, he was signing not only his own death warrant but that of his wife and children.

For the past twenty minutes, while bullets had sprayed all around, he had huddled in the shadows, strictly a spectator. But now the time had come to act.

Keller was not a particularly brave man. But now he had no choice.

Fitzpatrick's gun lay gleaming in the moonlight, a few steps away. A hundred fifty feet further away, the hard-faced man was getting into a car.

Keller stepped forward.

His fingers closed on the warm butt of Fitzpatrick's gun. It was, he noticed, a .38 automatic. He prayed it still had a shot or two left in it.

He straightened up. A hundred fifty feet away, the cold-faced man had the car door open. In a few seconds he would be gone, heading for Chicago and revenge.

"Hey, you!" Keller shouted. "Over here!"

The mobster paused uncertainly, before entering the car. He turned. He looked around.

Keller saw him as he stood in the moonlight—saw the cold, fleshless face of the man who so many hours ago had yanked him into a motel room and started this whole long night of violence. Keller raised the gun. He felt perfectly calm.

For Beth, he thought. *For Jeanie and Tom and the baby.*

He squeezed the trigger and a sound like a clap of doom exploded in front of him and a white hot pellet sprang across a hundred fifty feet of air and tore through a man's heart. The hard-faced man dropped without a sound. Keller smiled crookedly.

He let the gun drop from his hands. In the distance, police sirens finally shrilled. The nervous reaction came sweeping up over him, and Keller laughed hysterically in relief. The night of violence was over. Beth and the children were safe from gangland vendettas. Policemen were springing from their cars and advancing into the corpse-littered motor-court. Keller walked toward them, weak-kneed but happy, to tell them all about it.

The Final Crime Novel from
THE KING OF PULP FICTION!

DEAD
STREET

by MICKEY SPILLANE

PREPARED FOR PUBLICATION BY
MAX ALLAN COLLINS

For 20 years, former NYPD cop Jack Stang has lived with the memory of his girlfriend's death in an attempted abduction. But what if she didn't actually die? What if she somehow secretly survived, but lost her sight, her memory, and everything else she had…except her enemies?

Now Jack has a second chance to save the only woman he ever loved—*or to lose her for good.*

Acclaim for Mickey Spillane:

"One of the world's most popular mystery writers."
— The Washington Post

*"Spillane is a master in compelling you to
always turn the next page."*
— The New York Times

"A rough-hewn charm that's as refreshing as it is rare."
— Entertainment Weekly

"One of the all-time greats."
— Denver Rocky Mountain News

**Available now at your favorite bookstore.
For more information, visit
www.HardCaseCrime.com**